DADA
DATA

Jeff Bender

ISBN 978-0-9832512-1-7

I would like to thank the following people for their help in the
production of this book:

Sibyl Bender and Ellen Kyle
for the cover concept, design and artwork;

Tom Smith and Yvonne Daley
for their aesthetic support;

my wife, Lyn Drigert, and friend, Deb Thompson, for their
editorial eyes;

and Neal, Stan, Gypsy James and Frank
for their experiential guidance.

A Thumbnail History of Dada, Surrealism, Beatniks and Me

I was twelve or thirteen years old when I saw my first surrealist painting. I was looking through an art book in a seventh grade art class to stimulate an idea for a new project. The picture was Salvador Dali's "The Persistence of Memory." I turned the page and there it was, that great melting pocket watch draped over that perfectly cubic wall in an infinite nightmare landscape. The bizarre intensity of the painting tickled my imagination. My spirit flowed onto the page as if the painting was an aesthetic-genetic magnet for the creation-chromosomes of my sensitivity.

I was an aspiring Beatnik so I dug abstract art. My cousin and I dressed like Beatniks one Halloween. We hit the streets in our big berets and crepe paper goatees, slidin' into Coolsville with all our "hip" attitudes. We thought Beatniks were wild painters, sculptors, leotard-dancers and bongo-musicians in torn sweatshirts, berets, shades and goatees, drinkin' espresso coffee in dark basement rooms drippin' wine bottle candle light, listenin' to jazz, folk music and poetry through the smoky, down-beat, coffee house night. In my art classes, I wanted to imitate the different abstract styles I was discovering in my teacher's books; Cubism, Futurism, Expressionism, and all those other "isms" I thought every self-respecting Beatnik should know.

In high school, my Beats disappeared in the new beat of my Rock-an'-Roll. So, I tried to incorporate my understanding of their art without the guidance of the real Surreal literary masters hangin' out under streetlights blinkin' in the neon life of my art, illuminating alien landscapes orbiting my imagination.

It started in 1915 when a German poet, Hugo Ball, and his friend, Emmy Hemmings, migrated to Zurich to await the end of World War I. They despised and feared the war so they escaped the crumbling destruction of Germany to the neutral shelter of the Alps and gentle little Switzerland. They opened a nightclub called The Cabaret Voltaire, which became famous for the nocturnal art-antics of all the other young refugee intellectuals who had also gathered in Zurich to await the end of the Great War. They believed that the world had experienced collective insanity with its war-to-end-all-wars, and discovered their mutual loathing, disgust and distrust of society in general. They believed that the morals, values and institutions of society were no longer useful or functioning in the anarchy that ruled the day. They were angry, intelligent, young people hangin' around the city, thinkin' and waitin' with nothin' to do but kill time, examining the aesthetic by-products of the evolutionary wasteland of their experience.

They sought a new art that would express the deterioration of the existing self-devouring order. If the world was crumbling anyway, why not give it a shove? Destroy the old world and build a new world from scratch, constructed on a foundation of a more natural order rising, Phoenix-style, from the smoldering debris, to re-evolve a new sanity in the primal mud-swamps of humanity's industrial birth.

To find this art, they first had to rid themselves of all their preconceived notions of art. They believed that the popular art forms of the day, Bruitism, Cubism, and Futurism, were lies concealing the reckless destiny into which the world was hurling. A new art was needed that was a direct assault on society and no institution or perceived understanding was to be left untouched, and Dada was born.

The first Dada performances were held at the Cabaret Voltaire. The performances attacked the rules and conventions of modern order. There were paintings, primitive masks and collages by Hans Arp and Francis Picabia hanging on the walls. During the performances, Richard Huelsenbeck would beat a bass drum while Emmy Hemmings performed slow-motion acrobatics in a tutu as Hugo Ball, in a too-tall top hat, read one of his chant-like sound poems while Marcel Janko sang a popular song, pecking frantically on a broken typewriter. Then, Tristan Tzara, the Rumanian poet, would step to the podium and deliver one of his flaming Dada manifestos, or a lecture on modern pickle packing techniques.

The bar was packed every night with artists and curiosity seekers. Students and revolutionaries pushed together, drinking and smoking as the performance wore on.

After a while, the crowd became irritated and restless. They would boo and shout insults at the performers who screamed insults back at the audience. Riots broke out and the police burst in to break up the fights and make their arrests before they closed the place down.

When the bar re-opened, a week or two later, all the audiences and performers would come back and do it all over again. The riots weren't planned but became an expected vital conclusion to the performances, a desired response that served to punctuate what these Dadaists were trying to say. The performances were so popular that the troop took their show on the road to other cities and towns, a sort of floating Dada riot act proclaiming revolution against everything. Tristan Tzara said that if you were a true Dadaist, you despised Dada too.

Eventually, the anarchy of the movement took its toll and Dada came apart. The group became bored with the performances, which had become too predictable and expected, losing the spontaneous shock therapy they were designed to inspire. Dada was more, but the strong wills of the individual members of the group made it difficult for them to agree on which direction Dada should take. They argued until the war ended then took their Dada and went home.

In 1924, Andre' Breton, a long-time Dada poet, left the movement and published his first Manifesto of Surrealism. Breton proposed an art form he believed would express a new reality, a "sur" or "super" reality that was generated in the imagination by the juxtaposition of seemingly paradoxical understandings which, when placed in closer proximity to each other, generated a new truth in their union.

The technique that Breton suggested for tapping into these free associations of thought, was the technique of automatic writing; writing that was not directed by the poet's will but was rather, a result of a free-flowing record of mind continuum. In this way, new realities and associations could be revealed which had no basis in reason, and were therefore more natural and complete. Dueling forces could psychically bond, creating new unities of bioelectrical impulses flashing arcs across the great fissure dividing the brain. Other Dada painters and poets followed Breton and established Surrealism as a major force in modern art.

Breton was influenced by the imagery of the French Symbolist movement, particularly the prose poetry of Arthur Rimbaud and Issodor Ducass, "la compt de Lautreamont." According to Breton, the surreal image had to represent impossible beauty blending opposing forces of understanding. As an example of the imagery he invisioned, he used Lautreamont's image of a sensation as being, "beautiful as a chance meeting of an umbrella and a sewing machine on a dissection table" as the imagery he envisioned. In the contradictory terms of this image the imagination brings together sparks of inspirations spontaneously conceived in both the conscious and the unconscious mind at once. Life and death, past and future, reality and imagination, reason and passion; all exist in the same time-space continuum and cease to be contradictory truths, but become greater truths together.

The movement hit The United States in the '50's, through the Beats and the San Francisco Renaissance, particularly the poetry of Allen Ginsberg, Michael McClure, Gary Snyder, Gregory Corso, and Philip Lamantia; who, at the age of fifteen, was officially welcomed into the Surrealist movement by Andre' Breton; as well as the schizophrenic dream-prose adventures of William Burroughs. But, it was Jack Kerouac who promoted the use of spontaneous prose as a means of creating a free flowing record of mind wandering.

In her book, Memoirs of a Beatnik, Diane di Prima recalled her first meeting with Kerouac. He and Allen Ginsberg visited her apartment. They talked about poetry and Diane showed Jack some of her poems. She had changed some original words, crossing them out and replacing them with new words written above. Jack read them, crossed out the new words and wrote her first words back in; then told her to trust her original vision.

The movement reached me in a late-fifties, Jr. high school art class in Ohio, and after all these years it still trips my aesthetic switches. My words are embryos of a simple-celled organism of a wild species of literature I nurture. Synaptic insights fuse dreamscapes into places where everything is real and permitted. So, I submit this journal of reckless-romantic, random reflections of semi-automatic assault-rifle language riddling the void, as my contribution to the movement.

THE
RECKLESSTENTIAL
PAPERS

A Magician's Dance

Circles repeat discs of cultural visions. Original powers sail, floating like floppy Frisbees on winds that begin and return to the instant infinity of history.

A dark cave appears, a deep door in a glittering blue forest. A tall, thin, ancient man steps from the cave, spinning force-plates on crooked sticks. He glides across the forest floor in long robes. His wands draw light-rings under each plate. His eyes scan vast wooden skylines, iron seas and deep forests. Short brown men with armor and short swords expand from the east. Dark birds and beasts crouch and wait in mist-choked shadows of trees.

His arms whirl and release pastel spheres that float past spreading white-light waves emitting from his hair. He glides in silent rhythms of hemlock, ash, oak and fir. Spinning planets, moons and stars are talismans of whirlwinds sucked into and through the vacuum of his dervish motion. All shamanic tangents converge in that vortex, piercing the emerald flesh of trees.

THE KING OF SWORDS

When the movie started, the audience set their Cokes and popcorn down. Lights dimmed and the theater swelled with anticipation. A thick fog secreted an odor of sulfur and old meat; an acid mist emitted from the screen. In the beginning, the King declared war on everyone, believing the survivors would be assured of enough food, housing and power to go on.

Immense pillows of smoke rose to the massive head of the sky, spreading new-clear winter dreams of delirious nights that never melt. Children's eyes were split wide open. Wild hearts filled with black-light lenses of instamatic cameras focused on white-light cells of fear.

Some kids waited in the wings, watching the King. They had safety pins stuck in their heads. They sang streetlight knife-wound poems to the masses.

Warriors howled and flashed guns. The King was cloaked in the brutal soundtrack that droned in the background like an invasion of mute locusts.

Citizens recognized the pure survival tactics of rib-cage beasts in streets, praying for breath, flapping, out of control like broken reels spinning in the lobby. They burned smudge pots in the fields at night to shield the crops from the ice.

The King is dead. Long live his late-night reruns dissolving in animated water, scorched to steam driving a mechanical be-bop downbeat of fusion-light eroding neon-nightclub cities of sand.

LOVE AND INDUSTRY

Machine messiahs stalk oily surfaces of cities, soaring low, rattling over slumbering apartments on metal wings. A neon vortex of expressways curves out and up in a subatomic parabola of wild rockets, past smashed buildings at light speed bursting windows of bending rooms. Mechanical fingers sweep shards of glass eyes in, dusting the wavering ledge.

Naugahyde, cloaked and hooded priests circle, repeating sacred digital whisper chants to micro-ages of plastic chalices' circuits of electric highways' giga-goblets of synthetic palaces. Molten ceremonies of ground-zero intensity are performed. Smashed walls reassemble and breathe again. Concrete throats turn like mill wheels grinding as slow as a bootless soldier's retreat down a bruised and callused road. He flashes, pastel-khaki as he passes.

"Dogs' dreams! Dogs' dreams!" The princess screams, "I was only dancin' dogs' dreams around a sweet tower of marble beams' smooth thirst."

We met on a beach and burst in flames. Match heads scratched a concrete sky. The sun rolled red hours down the day. Shadow outlines shot sparks of comets from friction kingdoms of chrome-plated embrace. We slid sideways into peripheral visions of parking lots and guardrails along the way. Coral highways rushed like teacups floating in headlight beams splashing the edge of the road. Stars blinked and bobbed in gravel-waves slapping the concrete shore.

THE SPLATTER FACTOR

For Hiroshima and Nagasaki

The Flash

We have entered this city to measure the distance embedded between space-time and the way things were. Our party is small but ambitious. We will record the final eye's split blink.

Hot Clouds

Again and again I turn in a tight tangle of sheets. I haven't slept for days. I fear the shredding of my senses. This bright season was born in hot-pink clouds ripping a pastel slash in the sky. Footprints are embedded in molten concrete, two feet wide and deep. Shadows in relief, sacred symbols of a fluorescent sun, are pressed into and seared on the re-bar skeleton of the city.

Glowing air ignites the pale August morning. Flowers recoil in mountains. I squeeze their plump middles, their limp petals and metal fear. The radio is on all night, scratching like a static cat at the door. Stations run together. Heat bends. Light-ribbons slither in my shallow room. Coffee simmers on the stove in a low silhouette. Shadows repeat misty farewell kisses to the night.

The Priest

The war hangs from our necks like a rosary. We chant the great whore-names of industry in empty silo-temples. Our God, THEWARHEAD, is ticking. Automatic fingers poise on software hair triggers, quivering. Sweat beads on bowed heads of men.

A Ghost Dance

Splatter thermal eggs on your face, semi-clear and yellow. Splatter the ancient names of children with hot paste. The sky is glass. Bright smoke hangs over the flat center of a city, a twisted matchstick rubble-city of bricks and meat. Late-night windows rattle. Splintered heels are bone raw tendons pacing lead-lined rooms. The stateless winter night's necessity is more bitter than before. Cold is the pungent wind and swift, the subtle megaton delicacy of matter.

PERMANENT ANXIETY ATTACK

Late-Night Maintenance

When I'm afraid, I use a screwdriver to puncture the membrane walls of my skull with spaces that appear between silences. Heartbeats pulse like machine drugs I repeat. Thick, clear, neon voices crash in hot metal waves of breath.

Buildings blister. Bubbles pop in the fast-hand con-man voice of the wind. Flaming airwaves' fluorescent mists foam up, hanging textured tapestries over the sky. Cool colors embrace. Cities float on surfaces of puddles where pebbles drop, shattering and scattering diamond chips of light in the ripples.

The Desert

Oooooh, Oooooh, an incidental, but ever present, silence pervades the room. A desert spreads like a linen tablecloth on a white marble table before me. Platters of fruit appear in the hands of dancing girls who serve me in shear light skirts. They have veils over their faces and exotic jewels in their navels.

The feast begins; I listen to stories of old hooded men seated around fires in an oasis. Their tales draw me from my thirst. Music fades in hot winds. Men gnaw meat from charred bone.

Other men appear in glowing robes and return me to my thirst. Their stories construct cloud palaces in ancient

cities of sand. Music floats on corrosive winds' thin fingers
molding sandy streets with beggars attacking manic gates of a
shimmering city. Mobs kneel on hands and knees like pleading
lovers, parched lips pressed to the earth. In the desert, nomad
caravans cross the sand.

The Spider

In an uncharted childhood garden, a spider weaves
a shadow web, surfacing from nets to tangle tender legs
of children. Meat lives slap pavement in storms of leaves'
desperate directions. Faces have hands that cover tropical eyes
dissolving orchids and stars. Seek blood. Seek skin, veins and
muscle.

In case of permanent anxiety attack, don't listen to
any praying beasts hidden in leaves, entering skinned knees
of children on concrete venom-paths of play. In case of
permanent anxiety attack, blend with pavement, scraping knees
like a departing kiss thrown from full smooth lips ascending the
sanctuary of women.

Fish-stars orbit oceans. Silence is thick. I swim.
Churning legs mix Earth tu-tone blues swirling. Fine lines
vanish between sky and sea.

A Fish Story

A sticky black fish fell from a desert photograph of
the sun, thrashing like an oil slick at my feet. Its' grinding

leather gills were clogged with sand. Its' soft white underbelly scraped the land as it crawled, seeking liquid shelter. It gulped, anticipating hours' evaporating vapors of dust. Scratched marble eyes popped open, focused on the space between sand and water.

Oh fish of many colors, white rain is the sun's love. Seal me in liquid senses. Lay a thousand eggs in my eyes when I sleep. Between heartbeat's downpour of parched vision, throats open, choking, deep, dry and yellow.

The Paranoid Achiever

In case of permanent anxiety attack, crush glass with drumskin fists of feeble expressions. Stretch elastic bricks around the sky. Rebounding sounds come and go all night, overflowing ears with lush jungles gagging on overgrown altars and temples' calloused prayers folding.

On the seventh day we tested the gages and instruments we used to measure God's devotion. We calculated the angles of His perspectives, peering over bony shoulders of strangers in doorways, offering secret beasts to bar room arms of divine lovers.

THE BIRTH OF THE SIBYL

Frozen in a chrome-plated slow-motionless winter, impatient weeks pass, snapping teeth like famished animals, until a new dawn breaks over the mountains and uncovers a creation of miniature bones. Flesh and eggs accumulate like bio-dust on the windowsill of an antiseptic room. We are here to rest, eat, talk and sleep if we need to. The woman has draped herself in terry cloth scarves and robes. She crosses a private desert. A small sun beats in her womb.

I have come to this place to celebrate the night. I am the watchman of the sacred other-face of the moon, the recorder of tapes and tangents that converge and extend to the borders of old stars spreading like a fan, across the night, to cool sweat burning in the long squinting eyes of space. This is a woman's world. They gather to share their pain and watch each other, whispering and taking notes. They are monitoring the way life is forced from pink passages of ancestors. Crude picture-stories are carved on one-celled walls of flesh caves. They are the guardians of this room where our journey has begun.

When we were young, our footprints spread thin on the wind blowing through twisted streets we molded straight and smooth in our own image. We loved spending time turning corners and the way the city screwed-up in tight spirals and springs, and the angular way the sun scorched the shadows, and the shapes of the shadows as they stretched to touch our pain. We loved the length of time bending. We've discovered fire and invented wheels since then and reflexive smiles escape our lips.

The woman holds me, unraveling memory and reason. We walk. She showers occasionally in imposter rain, then drapes herself in scarves and robes again, for the parched land is calling. We breathe together in quick short bursts. I lean on her. She shines like a streetlight on the corner of humanity's main-street. Tires screech and spin souls, leaving rubber tracks on asphalt and snow, screaming through white geo-jungle ghost-streets ascending the concrete night assembled around us, brick by brick.

I smell fish in the jellied liquid that leaks from every pore in the woman's body. We are all born of flesh-sea, dragging slippery skin-scales across gravel, sand and salt, rising to the surface of the land. Waves touch us. Curling mists shimmer in the shade. The earth is barbed. Dry air smears a foul film on our bodies as we stretch tender scales to dry in the sun.

"Push past the pain," the women say, "we can see the head cresting, dark and deep as the shadows that cover your eyes." The woman moves beyond the invisible screen that separates our existences. I can't touch her when she walks, turns, runs again, then sits and jumps away from the tight walls that confine her.

Sleep is the heaven I'm seeking, contractions in time. Night closed in on us days ago. We will never go home alone. I watch the way the women gather around her with glittering eyes like jewels they give to her when they speak. An Aurora Borealis explodes in the northern sky. We can't see it; we only hear it fading in birth screams evolving from the woman's primal throat. Animals gather at the edge of the forest, cocking curious heads to listen to her pressing secrets howl.

Thin trails of red spread. The cave opens. Inverted towers toss a reckless earth, a wild eruption-earth shifting, expanding and opening fresh eyes of a new companion unfolding her arm's fluid wings, embracing the woman's weak, white, blood-stained and trembling thighs. Slime regenerates from her throat. Suction pores secrete thick, white, and sometimes sticky yellow water. Lives collide to stops in hallways. Steam billows up. Oozing heat radiates from the deep wet nest-bed where she lies. Rings of light eclipse glowing trees. Comets and stars streak the sky. The woman is finishing now. She walks no longer. She arches her back and says she has no time to see her life muscle pump the soft pink creature turning its head and rolling its wide eyes open from the vortex of her legs, attached to a blood-rope, a wet speck of earth erupting time and seasons. Slow bells clang shells three times. Dawn suspends crystal stalactites from a great white hole in the sky, as our new flesh-treasure squirms at the woman's side.

Needles in nipples, its time to feed the Sibyl again; drunk on milk of breasts, lying in the women's arms like a pink bouquet of flesh-flowers stealing fortunes from the careless hands of fresh inheritors of the earth, mouths laughing, stuffed with mothers' sweet skin.

The Sibyl is feasting on sleep now. Her head is nestled in the ancient pillow of my shoulder, mumbling her garbled sweet prophecies into my ear.

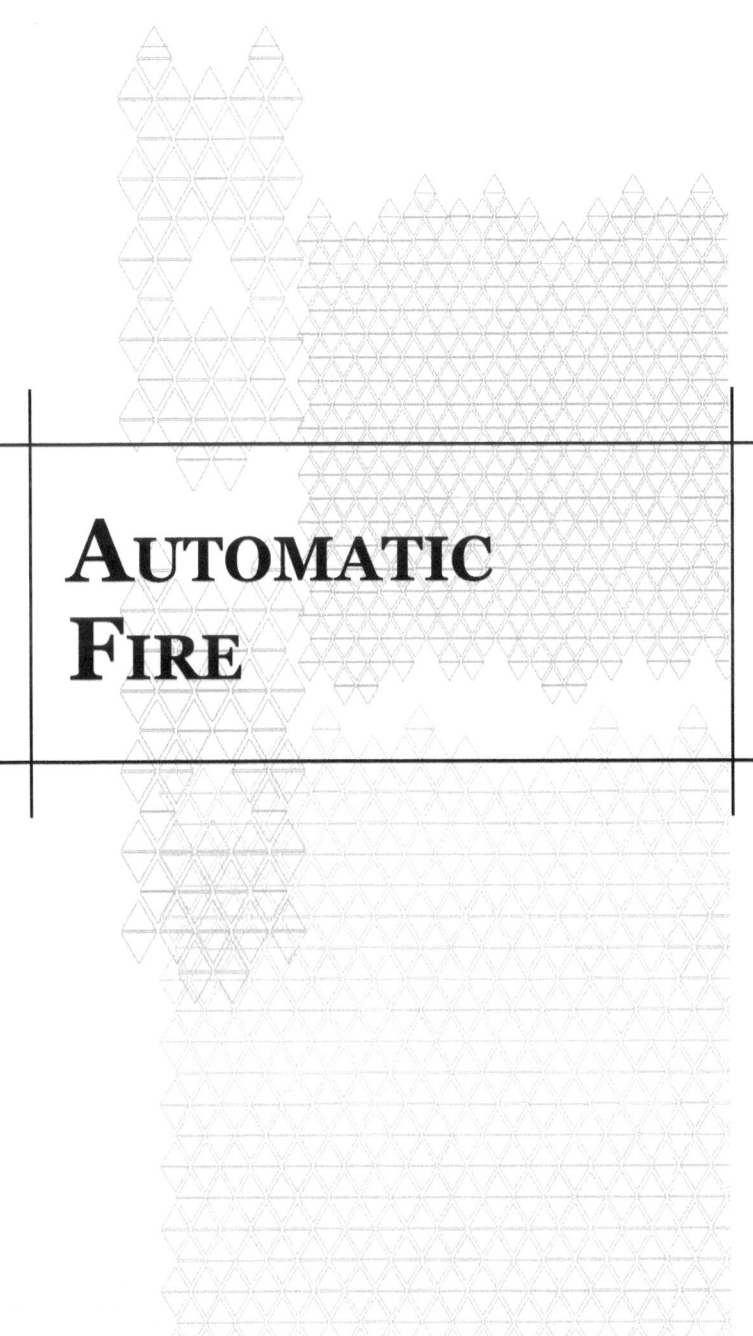

AUTOMATIC FIRE

SWITCHES

I never know how to begin. Mind fingers grope for just-right light-signs to aesthetic passages, as I fumble through my head for a switch to illuminate the way. I proceed like a stranger in an unfamiliar room, probing gray matter crevasses, seeking enlightenment.

I spread gray folds apart, digging down for any glittering illumination of the way. Sometimes, I give up on light and crawl all the way into those puffy folds, to mold darkness into Braille angels and demons. Gray-matter enlightenments emanate from black and blue temples of space.

SCENES AT DAYBREAK

Gray clouds shatter shards of night through the kitchen window, blowing away a hot pink light breaking over the horizon. Cars awake and approach the day in daybreak-dashes to important places to go. The cat is up, stretching and yawning, looking for food.

This house is a heat shield against the crisp air outside. The furnace pumps hums of heat, faithfully, sometimes.

Fall's comin' hard. I feel it in the stiff awakening of my bones to bitter collar-up days to come, starting frost covered cars with early exhaust-clouds rising to the brittle blue shell of the sky.

Time Waves

Morning is gray with a yellow tinge, foretelling a storm's coming or going. Static electrical build-up overflows a cup of thick air. In the autumnal shelter of this room, a universal state of disorder curls into itself, seeking balance in time-waves cresting and driving against distant sand and granite shores. Adrift on the season, washing up and sinking in its undertow, I am a skin-boat rising and falling in a great hurricane's whirling tail.

The cat contentedly licks his coat as I consider the depths and widths of the day, and the distances between instants, and the immense indifference of erupting galaxies. He curls up before me, assuming the shape of all non-things sucked into and through needle-eye storms rising in the east.

Autumn

Deep charcoal clouds fold into themselves, seeking balance. Leaves float like brown gulls dropping to drift above my sea-lawn, seeking sustenance circling beneath them. Rain paints morning with acrylic colors, brush-stroking roots and seeds. Death takes on a magnificent sheen in this autumnal dance of self-devouring order.

Wilted days of cold rain and leaves gone brown and falling down too soon, scatter on waves of sagging yellow grass this house floats on like a defeated warship after a battle, limping into port for repairs, shore leaves, loose women and glasses of ale to wash away the frosty dread of winter. Adrift, I sink and wash up in the undertow.

Sailors sing songs about adventures like these; salty fellowships of camaraderie and maritime addictions to distance, stars, and gale winds blowing through sun bleached flowing hair. Their women wander shorelines, awaiting passages to joyful homecomings, when men return to love's tender confinement, in kickback contemplation of a world without waves, even and still.

STRANGE METAL

This land is covered with frost. A furnace-sun grinds out heat from the basement. Seasons pass and earth forces collide like hammers pounding iron souls in the blacksmith hands of the universe, but I am a strange metal. I refuse to take shape. I circle and blend with perimeters of red and yellow leaves driven by winds from the north.

Ancient warriors drew bitter strength from this hard climate, huddled around fires. Hard faces examined dancing flames, matching that burning determination to their own headlong souls. Chromosomal strings connect us like relative puppets dangling from the bony fingers of space.

My grandchildren have entered my cave. They scream and laugh as if nothing exists but the instant wonders they confront, tickling their small feet and hands. They squirm in remote control sleeping bags of oblivious innocence, calling me to run with them through day's leafy dreams.

TEENAGE ROMANCE

Reptilian heads appear in a jungle of frost, white lizards of a snow-cracked earth. Vanquished grass sways. Thoughts drip with the coffee brewing in the space that fills this time. Whenever the void sings, I cock my hollow ears to listen.

Hummingbirds' wings hum. They have feathery little faces with beaks like straws stuck in adolescent mouths, sneering like black leather flowers in a fifties malt shop. Those were the days o' kickin' back after school and Mary Lou danced around the table, her pleated skirt risin' in the holy resurrection of her sweet white thighs of forbidden dreams.

Pagan rhythms rocked, drumbeat messages resonated from blackboard jungles and careful kisses in halls where monitors waited, assassins of the innocent tremors in the first starry eyes of love. What violence rang in those hidden bells? What glaring eyes slid into the seat behind you, clouded in such vengeful rage?

Boppin' down the block, the absence of those days opens like a dusty book on a back shelf of a wavering library. Between the pages, I am a before-and-after twin of a time-line sequence attached to both white ends of this continuum, stretched like a drumhead over a flesh-chasm of rhythmic hands.

FROZEN APPLES

This 6:00 A.M. rapier light thrusts and stabs the leafy landscape. Dark birds caw the sun up from behind pet-rabbit gray clouds breaking in slow motion glides to the horizon.

The dog barks whenever I startle his delicate sleep. Fears and threats slap the stillness of tender peace before the goals of fury. The cat left an hour ago. He stepped through the door and became a frozen black statue, casing the joint for any movement perceived through his instinct's eyes. Only his long slow tail moved back and forth, like a fuzzy radar sensor scanning for some dangerous or curious intruder.

Apples blister in the frost of this season, half rotten or too cold to rot, preserved until spring or until the winter deer find them in the crystal stillness of the night.

How frozen their flat black noses must be, rooting through the snow like that, but not as cold as the white-light smoke-flower cracks of undetected rifles kissing them with those red-hot-rendezvous lips of lead.

MIND SURFING

There are billions of miniscule pores in the flesh of the earth.

Masks cover children's faces condemned to journeys through lands where snakes and lizards catalog indifference.

Blue Jays with vulture's talons rip trees and bushes from the landscaped pavement of history.

Women wait in shadows with children dazed in sleep.

Match heads ignite like the startled heads of madmen or philosophers.

Electric daisies materialize in a great motherboard spring of matchbook changes.

Cats with kind eyes rub against the slow meat-clock of the morning.

Adorable little imaginings hang in the air, snail creeping across the desert length of day, laminating the vague surfaces of things with thin blue rain.

FOLK SONGS

Crows cry from mists that rise to hot pink cotton candy clouds swept by morning light. Slow cows roam the lumpy field across the road in a lazy motion.

The radio is on all night but I can't find any stations I like. Where are those sweet folksongs of peasant families fighting hopeless odds?

I remember too, those gentle-rebel Irish ballads, songs that blew like Druid-winds through that ancient emerald culture.

They used to play those heart-breaking sea shanties too, squeezebox jigs and sinking laments of treasures lost at sea.

APRIL MORNING

Dew-diamonds glitter on grass tips. A gray sun hangs from a heavy sky. Patti Smith twists dream-lyrics from the radio. "Gloria," and Van Morrison can't believe it. "Jesus died for somebody's sins, but not mine." I didn't say that. Where's she takin' this? G-L-O-R-I-A, yeah, but not this rushin' guitar slidin' slick-notes of grease and sweat."

Green and gray foghorns invade the morning. The radio's erupting blues now, clean-picked symphonies are played in hot-minute runs. The drummers hold it all together; iron hammers gleam in workers' hands poundin' a mean metal beat.

A Photograph Of The Fourth

Early rain dropped on an independent morning, drenching the sagging green cardboard facade of the landscape.

Tree-arms bang against the window, begging to come in.

A gray cloud ceiling of pressed aluminum is riveted to a cracked-tile sky.

Light blue and white gas and water hang from the sun.

Crow-songs break the silence, when no automobiles slice with jagged vibration, this canvas expanse of quiet fields.

When the cars blow by, they rattle the whole atomic structure of casual interlude.

I want to paint this picture with holographic colors in tiny boxes I place at the back of my eyes.

I want to sing this Gypsy deep-song of marvelous disharmony.

I want to play this instrument and dance on endangered stages of bars, beer halls, and smoke filled hangouts under black stars extinguished for forging the signature of the night.

THE DANGER OF BOOKS

Dreamscapes of rogues on the run from enforcers of laws and conventions are separate, hidden and removed. Even in a crowd, these guys stick out like some steel-shaving machine ravaging a primal forest.

Mad heroes zigzag sideways through schematics of lines on Harley Davidson's of thunderin' clouds corruptin' the quantum order of minute distances, in hot pursuit of some Elliot whimpering end; performing new Frankensteinian experiments on the poetics of flesh, brain scans, operations and transplants of art's neon anatomy.

TRANCE MISSIONS

BORDER LINES

Cloud-mist whirlwinds spin lust-dust along soul borders of mystery. Quiet wonders of fog-veiled understanding are perceived through shattered windows. Storms caress lovers' cheeks and pastoral landscapes. Wolves, hawks and squirrels harmonize in perfect-pitched food-chain melodies of satisfied holy hum. Horizons mix kaleidoscopic smear-shades. Breathing green fields, mountains and streams cascade sheets of gliding glimmer through the stoic nobility of trees.

The horizon is so wide and invisible. Opposites harmonize, collide, blend and revive, then collide again in an endless clash for dominance over the whirling. Misty rivers roll white-water books along the shore like rushes. Vast plains spread to mountains in clouds touching the sun.

I seek this place with great zest, focus and urgency, recording my encounters with opposing forces, and winning every battle. I have the stamina of wild-willed spirits and beasts. This is my party and I'll dance if I want to.

THE ASSASIN

Trails appear through a forest, categorizing and mapping the way.

Songs spring from bills of operatic crows cresting the sky.

Tribes gather to consult holy men on the best way to cross the wilderness before them.

The ringing silence is so clear it shatters sand's windowpanes, shredding tissue-paper images of a coming storm.

Dawn edges the corners of things in an orange light, exposing earth's leaking wounds to the sun.

A stranger crosses a dry flat plain, wrapped in a worn cloak trailing in the sand. He seeks the clean heat of the western lands; where scorpions, rattlesnakes, cactus and sagebrush stretch to the shimmering edge of the horizon. Behind him, dust rises in little tornado cones from his footsteps. His hypnotized eyes are fixed on the blurred horizon as he strides through the powdery wake of his passing.

HEARTS OF WONDER

I want to taste a mirage of liquid capes flapping, adrift in azure.

I want to watch the scent of chrome leopards racing against the backdrop of a steel blue jungle.

I want to lick a vision of broken blue eggs sucked clean by raccoons.

I want to smell mute crickets at dawn rubbing fabric leg songs of swish.

I want to peek into taut places of drum-lace rhythms and downbeats of second chances.

I want to kiss blind-side collisions with field mice running in wheels like old hamsters who's heads pop up, black eyed and peering, from sleepy childhood hearts of wonder.

LORCA IN NEW YORK

Lorca breathes soot-filled poems of industrial-strength brick-street machines grinding over the pages of his books like caterpillar tanks of birds.

Flaking flower-petal wallpaper is scraped from walls of peeling rooms.

Knife-fight melodies of revolver-crickets pop the night.

Delicate faces are wrapped in Gypsy reasons.

Political infidels kneel in barbed-wire allies or abandoned lots of revolutionary justice.

In the field across the street, the same cows Lorca saw still bellow and rush the horizon. Bobbing heads still butt the navy-blue cape of dawn.

NEW YORK MORNING

Honking geese crowd a pond in a park in Flushing, Queens. Random acts of soft-flight sink in milky wings of gulls and sad good-byes. Runners veer and yield to the careless flow of traffic. People walk along the edge of the park, hurrying, as if the last great stroll was at hand.

Sidewalks erase the union of pavement and grass spreading to crisp distance reflecting in cold black water. Brick-piles of living rooms are crammed together in crushing intimacy. Gray subways scream through tunnels of friction blending bright iron speed.

The Deadbeats

Winding engine's wheels and roads reduce sparks to platinum order. When the earth stops, I'll count railroad ties or watch TV for 24 hours; eyes open like plutonium atoms when high velocity neutrons come crashing in.

If everything were free, I'd take it anyway. It's my radioactive nature and health I must preserve, the glitter in my eyeteeth. In the end, I'll serve myself to space like a TV dinner I spent my life preparing, a charred feast of my birth.

Neal and Jack are in some kind'a car, Mercury or Lincoln maybe, light blue and white, chrome and sleek. It moves deluxe; 1947 hubcaps hover in the American desert. Mushroom clouds rise from back allies and radioactive dreams are sold in the street.

Neal and Jack are in China. They smoke opium in a desolate motel room and can't remember muttering perfect saxophone words in their sleep.

WESTERN RERUNS

The windmills of California revolve in a heavy tempest. Great towers with propellers strain to leave that place, where prairies meet Rocky Mountains in secret.

Vacuums of imagination freeze here. I start them early to warm them up and defrost their flat glass eyes.

Atmospheric repercussions echo like pool balls on a break when the eight ball hangs on the lip of a side cup, tauntingly vulnerable and threatening to leap.

Beside my coffee, a half grapefruit awaits initial hunger. Its seeds are split white and a pulp-stained knife lies at its curved yellow feet.

Relentless rodeos thunder through the mornin', jerkin' and jumpin', fire snortin' bulls and broncos dance hopscotch hooves around crumpled dumped bodies of cowboys.

SAND STORMS

A silk blue song slips from the radio and drifts like a negligee in a slow morning glide down tender pain. The snowstorm predicted yesterday petered out to a half-wet, deep-mess, tropical-winter squall.

I'm goin' back to the desert today to be cleansed in the hot winds of New Mexico. My song is my story. Kokopelli dances. Music curves from the humpback heat of his magic flute's soul ticklin' whirlwind sand-trips yielding to the heat.

ABSOLUTE ZERO

Mountains are blue-white horizons.

Brittle air shatters when I speak.

Degrees press down on the thermometer outside the window.

The silence of this morning after night-storm passed crackles; without antecedent, like a newborn ice-bird pecking at the crystal eggshell limits of winter.

The wind is even too cold to move, as if any motion at all will burn and stick to this sub-zero metal-pole day like a tongue.

Correspondences of fields and trees hang from the sky like signal flags of white transmission.

Frozen air peels flaking skin from atmospheric resistance.

Clouds cast a net-haze-weather-web across the sky to hold this cold day close.

THE MOVIES

"Lights, camera, action!" the director screamed at my birth, so I took the stage an' I been dancin' ever since. Boy, are my feet tired. I wanna sit down. Gimme five, man! I earned it! A cup o' Jo and a glazed doughnut wouldn't hurt either.

Isn't the band tired yet? The blisters on the guitarist's bloody fingers must be murder. How does he do it? All those high-pitched notes screamin' at right spots an' slidin' ta stops in all those perfect glides.

Look at those guys, millin' around. They can't wait to get started again, to enter music firin' feedback souls as I sit back and listen in quiet, born-again, break-time meditation on nothin' happnin' at all, but this bitter-sweet mornin' drenched in cold gray rain.

PLAYS

Spring's first buds pop-up tender green heads called from the earth, opening first-eyes to sun showering clean fresh faces with light.

The Tao moves un-clockwise through still moments. The job of time-flow is in its hands, and the only way to blend with it is through surrender. The ego-less faith required for fearlessness is a survival tactic of trust in the fact that chaos is just another undirected show, and each character is required to play a part, even when the theater's comin' down and broad heavy stage curtains burst into raging velvet walls of flame.

Slow Downs

Shudder-memories of lazy day beach trips, barefoot, shorts and no-shirt-kick-backs, glide to stops on hot shores of ancient lakes.

Pop-top heat-weights drip soft tar on back roads of summer quests.

Magnifying moments materialize and dissolve, caressing and pressing slow days down.

Hesitating blanket-wishes run on a reel, one frame at a time, meeting on midnight street-corners greeting dawn.

Mountains go on forever. Tandem, tarp-tied trucks glide down side-roads, hopin' the breaks'll hold or some uphill slow-down ramp'll reach out ta snag 'em like a coffee-cup truck stop along the way.

A Trance Of Lilacs

Lilacs drip in great profusion, popping from the branches of the bush outside the window. The lavender smell is so sweet and rich, it's almost too much to bear, like the taste of strawberry cheesecake, homemade fudge or pecan pie, too intoxicating to resist this butter-cream air of paradise.

I press my face in bulging blossoms.

Crows drift on the aroma of petal and beast.

Snakes, rabbits, and squirrels creep across the distance between the cycling flight of this time and the soft moist earth beneath my rooted feet.

Groggy pillow heads rise in twilight. Lavender impulses bloom and magnify a flower-laden light igniting this morning room.

GONE FISHIN'

I am a young boy lying in my bedroom with my big head stuck under my mattress, screaming at anyone who enters, "Whadda ya lookin' at? Get outta here! Go home! What the hell you lookin' at?"

I am a tiny man behind a small podium giving a nonsense speech in a monotone drone to a roomful of little empty chairs.

Moonlit landscapes open forests. People in evening dress are wild-eyed and silent when scavenger squirrels and crows enter, begging for food.

Summer is a hot plain of time to kill or revive like a waterlogged swimmer dragged from a lake, where trout, perch and bass watch and wait. Smooth black eyes hover above the water.

"Come on in." they say, "Join us. Grow gills, fins and a tail. Glide through wet perception, rising only when, and if, you wish."

NUMB
LOVE

DESIRE

Just because no one understands you doesn't mean you're an artist. You might be crazy, but that's okay. Where else can you do that better than art; writing, painting or sculpting your misperceptions and understandings of star-movement backwards, and oceans' evaporation of earth sweat condensed on the great freezer door of space, held open by the void and chaos, anti-glue of emptiness?

How can you reveal what you know behind a desk or counter, smiling and telling lies about the way you see things through your eyeteeth? Nerve endings direct your snarling vision-connection to places where synaptic wave patterns, arc lights of wild insights, chew and tear at realities of tooth and nail sustenance, force-fed conventions and politically correct reactions to abstract socialization.

Maybe you're not an artist, except in your own melting mind, but what a night-trip it's been. Put it down. Build your intensity around you, an aesthetic shield against the pounding mortar rounds of the official madness of fools.

All you wanna do is blow your harmonica like "Magic Dick" an' his lickin' stick, Sonny Boy Williamson, Little Walter or Allen, "The Blind Owl," Wilson. You wanna sound your sweet horn in a funky blues band so clean and bent to notes you only hear in your brain. So, you play by yourself on the porch, searchin' for sounds and one-hole pieces of heartstrings that cry. You play in fields on hot summer nights with the breath of stars and rustling tree branches vibrating the reeds of your instrument's blue soul. Notes rise from lives of shotgun farmer's families driven from their homes; deep, empty pockets, a little lint maybe, a few seeds, and your holy harp harvests their soul crops of steel rails clickin' freight train rhythms in the night.

THE BENEFITS OF
A CLASSICAL EDUCATION

An anxious clock is ticking time mechanics in a corner of my tongue. Three gears are grinding the elements of a sun-spoked morning rotating, counter clockwise, like a power train winding tight in my throat. Force is transmitted from my mouth. Motion or torque is changed.

Machine words pivot from my lips, loose language spit from the teeth as usual. The ratchet wheel slips. Stripped journeys disengage and prevent or impart motion. Parabolic thunder strikes the ivory air. Spontaneous gods of the seconds divide time for the fearful, rites for the spring-loaded holes in my solar plexus, where all my hot prayers slip into cylinders, raw sprockets and rings.

I am Socrates. I ask New Age megabyte questions. The worn out edge of my robe is torn and stained in smudged confinement. Pins and needles prick my skin and lodge behind my eyes. Pointy little headaches unravel threads of reasons used in the past to mend rips in fabric lives together again.

New novels, where the vanquished hero always wins, are written in the seams. Movies are made of them and replay in my head. Recycling videos fast forward and rewind tapes of boyhood day-streams spilling over the misty white cliffs at the edge of this page.

THE BOY

The skeleton passed from hand to hand; each eye and finger examined the luminous green bones. Maybe the remains of a lost polyurethane civilization dug up in some future history. There are white beads too, pearls worn for some special occasion, years ago, a wedding, a funeral or a first-date dance where a young girl met her first-love cheek to cheek, blending in one long memory.

Oh, the elegance of those smooth white balls hanging from her neck, where the silk breeze of his lips first brushed her tender skin. Oh, the goose bumps that rose in the cool heat of his breath, satin air folding her in love.

Other relics are un-packed; the little basket that held the tiny spring flowers she picked in the backyard of her childhood, the seashell she found that day on the beach when the ocean was too rough to swim in, but tempting her to danger at the end of her father's hand.

Her father taught her poetry and history in the everyday conversations and explorations they shared, road trips to then exotic places, Texas Falls, so common now in the shadows of the wonders of America but still packed away in her box of dreams.

Where is that boy, the one who tipped her heart so over into womanhood? She waits for him like a sailor's wife with only these plastic animals and people to occupy her time, until he returns to fill her again with his tales of conquered seas.

A Crap Game From Lorca's Barbarous Nights

"Seven come eleven fallin' out o' the sky, oh baby, daddy needs a new pair o' shoes." The crowd hushed as the dice danced, tumbling and rattling in the non-space between the shooter's rough sweaty hand, the pavement and the wall. But the dice rose, straight up, like ivory cubed alien ships to be kissed by the frost bitten lips of chance. They were seeking that black-dot pair of numbers where nobody wins, droppin' between the point's combinations and slippin' through probability's cracks, bold answers to vague questions that no one ever thought to ask.

When they hit, there is no sound. If dice fall in a greasy back-street alley in the dirty rain, behind trashcans and piles of shredded papers, garbage and piss, what are the odds? Do they make any sound at all, strikin' the wall and bouncin' back, if the bill-clenched cheerin' fist-crowd is gone?

THE DEVIL AND ARTHUR RIMBAUD

Subterraneans stalk lonely nights of hard solitude. If they fall, they fall alone then stand or perish, shielded by free will or analytical reason against passion-storms of reckless choices.

Rimbaud spoke to me from A Season in Hell. His foggy clarity was almost invisible in the clutter of time-collisions shooting stars, like slingshot-stones of mischievous angels hurled from the childhood back yard of space.

"Don't worry," Rimbaud said, "God'll put 'em to bed without any supper. He'll teach 'em a lesson they'll never forget."

"Forgive me Father," the angels say, "for bustin' the bedroom window of the world. I was just goofin'."

Rimbaud laughed when he told me this, but a black hole glint flashed in his pale blue eye, cuttin' heads like a New York Blues boy on the road to Robert Johnson's crossroads, to beat the Devil's feedback-protégé in a blazin' blue guitar war, escapin' the electric heat o' the music with his Mojo-Hand left un-scorched by the flame.

A Song Of Maldoror

Ducasse sits in a cold Paris room wearing proud rags.
Cruel words fall onto the page, silent as snow dripping from
branches of willing pines, quiet harmony of matter, gravity and
wind.

Isidore, le Comte de Lautremont, sings Les Chants
de Maldoror. His rags become knee-high black leather boots,
tight velvet pants, satin sash, embroidered white design on
ebony sheen, white pirate shirt of knife fight shadow-poet in a
red silk waistcoat and cape.

He eats with grimy fingers, cat, rat and dog flesh from
a cracked bowl on a rough wooden table. He sits on a warped
wooden chair staring at the bare walls of his room, the small
chest of drawers or stained naked mattress and thin blanket on
sagging springs in the corner. His gaze drifts to his little stove.
There's heat when there's wood. He wipes a greasy hand on
worn wool trousers and picks up the page he's written.

Rioters rage through the city; impoverished masses looting
and killing, worn men and women, bare-footed grubby children.
Men carry heads and testicles of the new nobility impaled on long
poles in this revolutionary parade.

Ducasse watches through the grimy glass of his
little window. *The poor are always angry*, he thinks, *but
usually too sick, tired or hungry to fight.* The crowd passes.
Crumpled leaflets of mob demands litter the wind swept street.
Bloodstains smear in snow.

GHOSTS OF THE ROAD

Mad motor hot-rods scream down this high school, highway get-a-way night with Bob in his parents' new Bonneville station wagon, big engine overload of accessories, road rocket with padded seats and deep plush carpet. Smokey an' the Miracles' moan "The Tracks of My Tears" on the radio. We stop at the Big Clown Drive-In, outside o' town, for some burgers, fries, and shakes. "Louie, Louie" blares from another radio, when Joe, my girl's ex-boyfriend, sees us and chases us down a country road in his friend's muscle-motor Grand Prix in a rage of teenage love.

I don't want Joe to catch us. He beat-up the meanest Hood in school and left him twitchin' in a pool o' blood; a red blob lyin' like road-kill at the side of some back road. Joe sat on the guy. He grabbed him by his long blond DA wings and smashed his head into the pavement. His friends had to pull Joe off before he killed the guy.

Bob's left arm rests on the open window. I control the radio. Rolling Stones, "Not Fade Away," I crank it up. Bob steers with his right hand, blond crew cut and rolled-up T-shirt sleeves like a Marine with a cigarette clenched in his teeth; a hundred miles an hour with Joe and his buddy right on our tail, cruisin' headlong into that dead-end T in the road flyin' in our faces.

Bob doesn't slow down a bit when he hits that T; he just locks up the brakes and cuts the wheel to the left like Steve McQueen slidin' on a dime into that ninety-degree direction we were seekin'. He cuts the wheel too far though and we spin three doughnuts across some farmer's front lawn. Joe and his buddy bounce right by. Bob turns the wheel to the right and the Grand Prix just misses the rear end of the wagon spinnin' out of the way, in an automotive greaser-ballet that couldn't have been choreographed or performed any better.

Turnin' to a stop, the nose of the Pontiac points down the same road we just came in on. "She's real fine, my 409," the Beach Boys sing, along with the hum of the engine, still runnin', so Bob peels-out across the lawn and down the same road we just came in on, in the final lap of our Great Escape.

THE GATHERING

Two unexploded firecrackers with quarter inch fuses lie on the windowsill. They didn't go off on the Fourth of July. I've been waiting for the right time to ignite them and run away before they blow. That's about the extent of my adventure this summer. Last summer I was on a joy ride across America. I'm home now, doing roof, ceiling and shelter things to improve the conditions of my family's survival. Maybe I'll do that sweat lodge next week with Neal and howl like Robert Bly in the forest, seeking my warrior soul in the company of steaming men.

I did that in the seventies at Woody's hand-hewn log cabin farm in Middletown Springs. Woody and his friends, a gang of outlaw back-to-the-landers, lived outside of town. Woody built the place with old hand tools out of logs he cut down and dragged from the woods with workhorses. He built a cabin with a loft, a barn and two smaller sheds. The place looked like a hundred years ago, complete with mountain men and women, and kerosene and wood power.

They built a log sauna behind the cabin, a Sweat Lodge where they gathered naked on winter nights, lounging on wooden platforms around a barrel stove with rocks stacked and piled on top in the corner. They dropped sizzling snowballs dripped with exotic scented oils onto the hot stones, producing clouds of fragrant steam in the small log room. They stayed in the lodge and absorbed the heat until their bodies glowed through every organ.

They sat cross-legged on the platforms, chanting in ancient warrior tongues until they could bear the heat no longer and hobbled from the lodge into the night, to dive headfirst into the moonlit snow, screaming and awakening every non-sense at once in crystal surrender.

MORPHEUS

You have a lifetime of tunes tucked away in the shifting wrinkles of your brain, each piece connected to a tender focal point in time, and the older you get the more your music sings. It doesn't have to be bright an' boppy to bring ya up. Some low down, tear jerkin', soul will do; 'cause, no matter how bad ya feel, if it wasn't for bad luck, Smokey wouldn't have no luck at all tracin' the tracks of his tears.

Maybe you wanna hear some soft guitar glides; John Fahey's mystical American folk sound slidin' twangs plucked and picked so fast you forget your blues and wonder, where's he find all those notes an' how's he hit 'em so fast?

Nina Simone sings sweet songs from Porgy and Bess, "Summertime an' the livin' is easy, fish are jumpin' an' the cotton's high." Her sweet voice takes you right down that rollin' river to places so fast and wet they only exist flowin' under your riverboat of Tom an' Huck fishin' pole dreams.

Sometimes you find the recordings you like in music store discount bins and unpopular tune-racks in the corner. Other times, you gotta order 'em an' wait; a couple o' weeks maybe, when all you wanna do is hear it now. So your kids show you how to download music online and you go nuts with the possibilities. How do you prioritize? Fifty years of music's jammed in your head. You knew your machine could sing a long time ago but you didn't know how far it could go. You do now and you can't get enough. Endless strings of titles scroll before your glazed eyes. Notes flash inside; hot rod piston-glides ignite enlightenments of mathematical intimacy.

The kids say, "We had this all the time dad, why ya getting' into it now?"

"It takes a while," you say. Then you spend the day copyin' songs to CDs and the kids don't get the computer 'til way past midnight.

THE MILLION-DOLLAR QUARTET

Johnny Cash died in a Memphis hospital last night, followin' Elvis, racin' in a '57 Chevy to rock n' roll heaven through a burnin' ring o' fire.

Jerry Lee, The Killer, waits for death, stool kicked back, leanin' on a flamin' piano rememberin' Memphis. Great Balls o' Fire roar from his poundin' strings and keys to blue highway horizons touchin' the sun. "Come on over baby, whole lotta shakin' goin' on."

Chrome tears stain Carl's blue suede shoes.

Jitterbug dance steps gyrate hips too mean to be seen, rumblin' white kids' souls with black forbidden rhythms, mad guitar licks and drumbeat rough songs of tough times and trusted lost loves of young America. Sweet-treat white chocolate tunes spoil kids' appetites for post war Levittown homes with new ranges and Frigidaire's in every one.

Wives of discharged sailors and soldiers raise kids to be hot rod rebels, space travelers, protestors an' military invaders, A-Bomb an' H-Bomb cultivators of mushroom cloud-gardens risin' from the duck and cover fears of the radioactive earth. Dads chase prosperity at any price.

Live TV can't cover mistakes. Transistor radio signals fill teenage ear-plugged ears with the Rock-a-Billy black beats of Johnny and the white rockers boppin', in secret, under the downbeat bedtime sheets of the night.

GRAPES OF WRATH

Woody Guthrie sings gray songs risin' to the shimmerin' edge of the atmosphere. Clouds flow from fixed nostalgia-streams of ancestral memory. God's tongue grooms the earth like a mother-cat tending to her young.

The light is so thick, I touch and smooth its physics-fur to the glass flesh of the waiting spring. I move through reluctant mornings, gathering ripe fruits and berries from thorny vines. Pastel petals fall and shatter the howling silence.

Tortured dust is my cellmate, condemned to the same parched prison as the earth. Homeless farm families seek elusive crops to pick, clinging to the great motherland, which is at once their clear birth, death and small existence in purple valleys of proud and defiant mountains and wilting trees.

Reflections in the mirrored walls of my skull glitter like chrome handles of old vending machine candy calling through posted glass.

"Them's two fer a penny," the waitress said, placing the sticks of candy in the children's hands. The truck drivers teased her soft heart over their coffee.

"Hey, dose ain't two fer a penny, d're a nickel a piece."

"What's it to ya?" she said, eyes open to roads' illusive last runs.

"Hey! Wait a minute! You got change!" She shouted, as the drivers tossed her their money and walked through the door.

"What's it to ya?" one snapped, smilin' in a tender-tough gesture that stretched like a late afternoon shadow across the truck stop myth of America.

ROAD TRIP

Subways click to greasy slow-stops in this city of fast scenes and cars. Highways fly by. Dotted lines perforate the asphalt. Landscape smear-shades of blue-green and gold pass in a blur of speed, each instant a complete whole, each foot of the way. Roads rip the friction of speed bumps in the land rolling over continents, speed against light speed and shadow like the shifting line where they meet gray pavement.

The road behind disintegrates into static energy of passing light through skin, stretched over time-lapse sequences of headlight eye-cones piercing wavering horizon shades of green, tan, and brown mountains. Forests and seas lap the earth at the end of the land. The road whines and shines like a glass rail of a cloud-train. Talking Heads on the radio peel dead skin from the pavement.

"Truck Stop Ahead," last Chance Texaco before you enter the fire-wind land you're crossing. Last chance to turn back before the barrier land between dreams. The sun is hot; pumping gas ignites in your hand. You gaze into blistering souls of sunburned roadsides along the way, shimmering in a ghost-dance mirage fading in the sand.

Inside the station, in the sweaty shade, a young native woman looks through binoculars to read the amount you owe on the pump. No digital readout in the close dark room, too hot to walk in the sun. "That'll be twenty-two fifty," she says, eyes and hair black as midnight in the charcoal shadows of the station's dim light.

ELKO NEVADA

"Hey man! Howya doin'? I seen ya sittin' here from across the street, thought I'd come over. Hey, you gotta smoke man?

"You remember me? Yeah, you do. I know you from 'bout a year ago. Remember? Hey, you gotta light man?"

"Where you from anyway? You ain't from around here are ya? You're a long way from home, huh? Come on man, you know me, say no an' your eyes lie."

"Ya see man, there's this little place across town I gotta get to and you gotta big van man, maybe you could gimme a lift, you know, just across town. Whadda ya say?"

"Listen man, I see you. Your soul's an empty wine bottle rollin' in the street. Hey! Don't you look away! Don't you dare look away! You look at me now! You know me, yeah, you seen me 'bout a year ago. Say no and your eyes lie!"

Sometimes, all you can do is stop for thunderstorms in poor desert towns and sit in your van, smokin', waitin' for your wife and kids pickin' up some food. You stare at the desolate image of the side street where you're parked. It's poverty is a faded thread woven through the desperate condition of the flesh stained tapestry of America, an' all you wanna do is get your stuff and go.

A stranger breaks the plains of your space and you're invisible no more. He's big, bear chested and drunk. He wants a cigarette. You oblige him. You want him to leave but he stays. You sense danger but you don't know if your fear senses are real or imagined, so you don't know how to respond. A defensive state-of-mind for sure, but should you attack to gain the advantage? Your instincts whisper, "No," but your desire to survive is screamin', "Get 'im before he gets you." He says he knows you and recognizes your lies. He asks for a ride and you refuse. He gets more indignant and demanding. Do you strike or wait, or just step around his spear-tipped eyes and listen?

"Okay, later man, I gotta go. Oh yeah, you got any change?"

THE BAR

Listen man, I was just sittin' in my van outside a run-down Grand Union on a dirty back street of this little desert town. I stopped to wait out the thunderin' storm-beat threat o' severe weather. Electric flashes cracked in the sky, so I checked into a cheap motel room for the night and had a few beers in a little country bar across the street.

I was smokin' a cigarette, studyin' the beat-up little place, pool table, saddle blankets, and leather gear hangin' on the walls, workin' on a shot 'o Jim Beam an' a beer, when this cowboy walks up. He had dark skin, black eyes and thick black hair. He was heavy set, shirtless, leather vest and wearin' a pair of dirty black jeans. He was drunk. He shoved me on the shoulder an' said, "You got a smoke man? Whadda you looking' at? You like me or somthin'? You must like me. You been starin' at me since ya walked in. Whadda ya want man?"

"I don't want nothin'." I said. No trouble anyway, that's for sure; besides, three of his greaser buddies were leanin' on the other end of the bar. I got nothin' against Mexicans or Indians, you know. They ain't in my way or anything, we're just different's all. But I wasn't gonna take any lip from 'im either.

I handed him a smoke. His eyes were onyx-tipped spears. He was agitated but settled down. He seemed calm, drunk and friendly. Then he grabbed my shoulder so I smashed

'im in the face with my bottle. He backed off, blood drippin'
from his cheek. He wiped it off, sneered an' attacked. I'd 'o
been okay but his amigos jumped in, so I ran out the door.
That's all that happened officer. I didn't do nothin', I didn't
call him nothin', an' that ain't my knife.

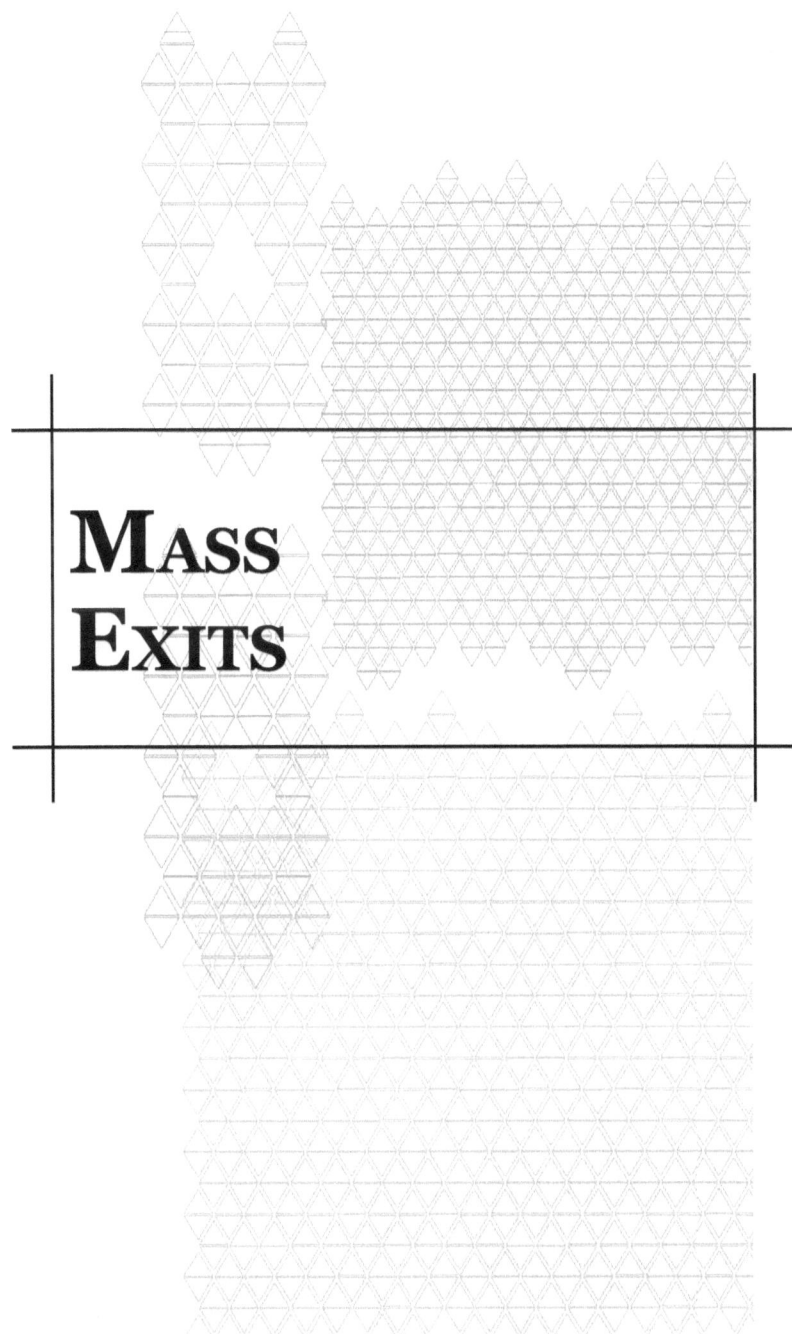

MASS
EXITS

45 R.P.M. Balloons

I am six or seven years old, sick at home with Scarlet Fever. A deep burning itch radiates from a hot red rash on the inside of my wrists. The rash torments me until the endless irritation is almost too much to bear. Calmly delirious, I burn alone under a blanket on the couch in the living room with my father, mother and sister nearby. They walk around and talk like spirits from another dimension that I glimpse on the blurred edge of my vision. They speak an unknown language, which I also speak but do not understand. I only participate in the conversations because they are my family. I am alone but not lonely, and perfectly content to lie and bake in the heat of my private madness.

Because I'm sick, my parents play my .45 R.P.M. records for me on the family hi-fi. Usually, my sister and I are not permitted to play our records on the hi-fi, but this is a special occasion. My records are the Looney Tune adventures of Bugs Bunny, Porky Pig, and Daffy Duck. I love their madcap antics and listen to them often on my little record player in my room. I am enjoying my delirium, watching the hi-fi in the corner as my records play, when one of the records blows up like a balloon and floats out of the open top of the stereo to the ceiling.

One by one, more records blow up and pop out, gradually expanding to fat black balls with fat 45 R.P.M. holes in the middle, surrounded by bright red, green, blue, and yellow labels. Balloon records float up, bumping and bouncing against the ceiling. I am filled with wonder at this sight, for this balloon-dream seems so right and natural, like a time-lapse flower blooming, an erupting orange sunset diminishing and going down, or the slippery green flickering of spring leaves dancing with rain.

DENTAL HEALTH

I'm a young boy walking down the street with my mother. We're going to the dentist so I can have a tooth pulled. I'm in the dentist's office following a nurse down a long corridor to a small back room. I sit in a big black leather chair with a chrome handle attached to the side. Weird mad-scientist gadgets and machines surround me. A stainless steel tray filled with dozens of curved and pointed tools sits on a small cart beside the chair. Chrome steel and black rubber robot arms hang over my head. Thin metal cables are woven through little pulleys attached with bolts and bearings to the joints of the arms. A white porcelain sink rests at my left elbow. Clear water streams from a short chrome tube protruding from just under the lip of the sink, swirling in a whirlpool through a thick black hole in the middle.

The dentist stands beside me. He pulls the handle of the chair, lays me back and leans over me. He has a neat gray crew cut and a bristly gray moustache and goatee. Black horn-rimmed glasses rest on his nose. His doctor's jacket is too starched and white. He smiles with a mouthful of big white teeth. I look around. From behind, the nurse places a cold black rubber mask over my face that covers my mouth and nose. I struggle to push it away but the dentist and nurse are bigger and stronger than I am. They attach the mask to my head with elastic straps that hook in the back. I'm afraid I'll suffocate. The dentist turns on the gas.

Bitter metal air fills my lungs. My eyes close. My head pounds. I spin through a funnel turning bright points of stars to metallic colored flakes piercing a rolling backdrop wavering in a sheet-metal night, curling into a whirling cone through which I fall. Vibrating heavy metal gongs pound in my head. Soul sparks shoot through raw nerve endings screaming from my skin. A fuzzy, hot-pink rubber cap covers the thin shell of my skull.

My eyes open. I'm walking home with my mother through another groggy-dream. I don't even notice her until we're there. We enter the house and go directly to the kitchen. She mixes a glass of warm salt water at the sink so I can rinse the blood from my mouth and heal the tender hole in my jaw where my tooth used to be. I can't concentrate. My spirit is drifting. Dad walks in.

I see him as I saw him about half my life before, coal miner in West Virginia, black smudged face and clothes, dark hard helmet with a light in front. Only his eyes and teeth are white. He is smiling.

He smiles again as he walks into the room, but a dull drunk-smile this time. I see it in his eyes. His clothes are clean. He's lean and muscular in a short-sleeved shirt. My mother sets the glass of salt water on the table. She and my father argue over the car keys. He holds her off with one hand while he takes the keys off her key ring with the other. She is crying and beating his chest with her small white fists.

"I want my water!"

"Let me go!" My mother screams. "He needs his water!"

"Okay" Dad says. Then he grabs a glass from the cupboard, pours some salt in and turns on the spigot, filling the glass with cold water. The pressure is too hard. Rushing water spins and spills out over the top. Dad grabs a spoon. He jabs it into the glass and stirs. The spoon tinkles against the side of the glass. Metal rings spin in a small whirlpool in my father's hand as he reaches through the vortex of the pinwheel kitchen-fan and hands me the cloudy glass. "Now go to the bathroom and rinse," he says.

THE BABY

My wife and I are racing down a highway in the middle of the night. I am driving. She is holding a sick baby. We are headed for a hospital. An atmosphere of dread permeates the car. It isn't our baby, but it's our responsibility. The road is wet and slick but straight, no traffic in the way. We come to a steep downgrade. I keep up my speed because the highway is clear. I notice three tractor-trailer rigs stopped at a crossroads light at the bottom of the hill. I pump the brakes. They are mushy. I can't slow down. I'm outta control, flying headlong into a flaming steel disaster. I manage to avoid each truck, weaving between them, barely missing each, until I skid sideways into a rest stop at the side of the road. The car tips up on two wheels and almost flips over but gravity pulls it down before that final death-dance dip of crushing metal and broken glass ends our trip.

We stare at each other, wild-eyed. She clutches the baby. We have to keep going but can't chance it without brakes. I climb out of the car to see what's wrong and discover that the brake mechanism is just a worn out rope running through a series of small pulleys attached to various spots on the floor, driver's seat and dashboard. The rope, which had been sequentially woven through the pulleys, is lying limp and unraveled in a small heap on the floor. I don't know how to restring it, where to begin or what pulley-order to weave it through. There are dozens of pulleys and the rope needs to be woven in a certain order for the brakes to hold.

I try many sequences but nothing works. The urgency of the situation grips me like a fist. Five or six drivers from the trucks stopped at the light walk over. They say they know what the problem is and can fix it. I'm grateful for their help and allow them to work on the car. I step aside as they dive in, asses and elbows flyin' as they restring the rope. When they finish, one guy says, "All set buddy. Climb on in."

I glide into the driver's seat but ropes run in all directions crisscrossing the whole inside of the car, through pulleys that hadn't even been there before. New pulleys are attached to the front seat, back seat and ceiling. Pulleys are even attached to my wife and the baby, and the rope is laced through them in some mysterious web of mad-brake technology.

"Shove on in Buddy. Try 'er out." He says.

I punch him in the chest. "Are you crazy? What'd you do? I can't drive this! Get outta here! I'll fix it myself!"

The guy comes at me and we face off. He stops, then the other guys walk him back to the trucks. I unlace the rope and try to re-lace it again. Then, my son appears in a mist. I'm surprised to see him. He killed himself a few weeks ago. I thought he was dead. He reaches into the car and over my shoulder to help. "Let me try," he says. "I'll fix it."

I shove him hard in the chest with my elbow and scream, "Get outta here! Leave me alone!" He's lying on the ground. He stands up and crouches low, snarling in a vicious smile. A fiery glint flashes in his damp eyes.

"I ain't gotta take this no more!" he says.

I wait, frozen in the instant. He wants to take me down. I see it in his eyes. "Go for it," I say, " show me whatcha got."

DANIEL AND THE HOLY GUN

Daniel and I were lost in a blue forest. A thin layer of silver blue pine needles glittered in the pastel blue light of an unseen moon. Tall trees lined the sides of the path, outlined in moonlight radiating charcoal shadows against the black forest beyond. Unsure of our location and unaware of why we were there, I felt an instinctual need to move on. The night was a black velvet cave we passed through on a path as wide as a backcountry road. The path narrowed as we walked, and the further we walked the tighter the blue forest pressed in. We pulled machetes from sheaths that hung from our belts and whacked our way through the gray underbrush. There were no stars. Tree branches had closed in over us, blocking out the sky. I could only see, for a short distance, thicker branches hanging like charcoal shades over the window of the night.

A powder blue clearing appeared, a circle of pale blue light edged in shadow. An old stone arch stood at the near end of the clearing. It looked like the Arch de Triomphe in Paris, but was only about four feet tall. We followed the path to the arch. Hieroglyphics and mysterious symbols were carved in weather-eaten stone. I knelt down to crawl through and saw a gun, a silver revolver with a pearl handle lying in the shadow of the right leg of the arch. I picked it up. It looked like a gun from the nineteenth-century American West. The silver was tarnished but not pitted. The pearl handle was bright white, not yellow, chipped or broken. The gun was designed to break open at the cylinder for loading. I opened it. The inside surfaces of the cylinder and handle turned into a gaping red mouth stuffed with a fat red tongue choking in a smothered scream.

The gun jerked in my hand, coughing and gagging in violent spasms. I looked down its throat. With each anxious gag a small pink creature appeared, tumbling up, out, and over the gun's tongue, teeth and lips. They were puffy, almost featureless, little embryos of a four-legged animal. Pointy ears stuck up from round little heads, lash-less eyes were closed above short blunt noses. Their mouths opened and closed in a desperate suckling motion as they squirmed at our feet. The creatures fell from the gun until they covered the ground and clogged the opening of the arch. I dropped the gun and looked for a way out. In my mind's eye, I saw a cliff a few yards through the trees and yelled, "Daniel, gather your ropes, we gotta go! There's a cliff about fifty yards through those blue pines. That's our way out."

We removed our ropes but discovered that they were only short lengths of rope tangled and knotted together in a roll, and none of the pieces were long enough to rappel a cliff. "Tie 'em together Daniel! We gotta go! Make it snappy!"

We knelt down and tied our ropes together as the pink marshmallow creatures continued to spill from the spasmodic mouth of the fallen gun. "Get movin' Daniel. Tie faster. Let's go!"

"I'm goin' as fast as I can. Whatta ya want from me? I only got two hands."

"Well don't be so picky. We gotta move! We gotta go!"

The little pink embryos continued to belch from the mouth of the gun. They covered the ground and tangled in the ropes as we worked. They were so thick, we crushed many of them under our feet as we moved around. "Come on Daniel, grab what ya got an' follow me. It's over here."

We gathered our ropes, ran into the trees and found a cliff, just as I had seen it. It was a granite ledge at the edge of the woods descending into darkness. I looked back to see if the little pink beasts had followed. "Daniel! Tie one end of your rope to that birch tree over there, and throw the other end over the cliff. I'll tie mine to this little pine, we'll slide down as far as we can and hope for the best."

We secured our ropes and slipped over the edge, struggling and kicking, bashing knuckles and knees on sharp stones jutting from the cliff wall. I reached the end of my rope and dangled in the dark. I couldn't see the bottom so I didn't know how far below us it was. "We gotta climb back up Daniel. I can't see anything and I don't know how far down it drops."

"I can't hold on any more."

"Yeah, ya can Daniel. Ya can do that an' more. Come on, we gotta climb."

"My arms, man, I can't do it."

"Ya can do it. It's better than droppin'. Just put one hand and foot over the other 'til ya reach the top. We stand a better chance against those little blobs than we do droppin' into this void. We're bigger than they are. We can take 'em."

Rocks I gripped and stood on crumbled under my feet as I climbed. Daniel struggled, "Keep movin' man. You're doin' great." I said. My fingers and knees were raw and bleeding but I climbed until I reached the top.

I peered over the edge to see if there was any sign of the embryos, crawled up and over on my belly, then stood up and helped Daniel. We rested, then made our way back to the clearing. The gun was lying in the shadow of the arch where I found it. The cylinder was closed and all the pink embryos were gone. We pulled our sleeping bags from the packs we were carrying, spread them out then climbed in and went to sleep. Soft stars draped a shear blue curtain over the black window of the sky.

When I awoke, a pale blue sun rose over a navy blue meadow at the far end of the clearing. A cabin appeared in the center of the meadow in a cluster of thinning trees. It was a cozy little place in the morning mist. A young woman and a girl lived there. The woman was tall, strong, thin, sleek muscled and graceful like a deer. Her dark hair glittered when the wind lifted it from her long white neck. Her eyes were quick, bright slate blue discs floating in the milky pools of her cheeks. The girl looked like a younger version of the woman. They could have been mother and daughter or sisters, they looked so much alike, or before and after photographs of a girl child grown to woman.

Days passed in a whisper. I wanted to go but Daniel and I took great comfort in the way the women moved through their lives like elemental spirit-spheres swirling in the meadow. Daniel and I had been friends for many years and had shared many adventures. Usually, I was our leader but this time I had no idea of where we had been, where we were, where we were going or why, or how to get there, so we waited.

Daniel was tall and lean with a medium build. He had dark brown curly hair that covered his head and neck like a woolly helmet, and a thin black moustache and goatee that gave him the look of a lecherous imp. His eyes were black wild fires. When he smiled, his eyebrows rose to two points like tee-pees above his eyes, stretching a stack of skin Vs resting on the bridge of his long thin nose. When Daniel saw the women though, he became infatuated, blinded and sucked into a trance tunnel of love, hypnotized in laser enchantment.

"Daniel, we gotta go. We gotta get back." I said, although to what, I did not know. He remembered our journey. It just wasn't important anymore. As he watched the women, his bright black eyes became two light blue crystal balls like the eyes of an angel or a holy man on a quest. His face was bright, soft and warm, no wrinkles. He stood up and crossed the clearing into the meadow with steady focused steps until he reached the door of the cabin. He knocked. The women greeted him with smiling faces and invited him in. They fed him supper and he stayed the night. In the morning, they awoke before dawn, ate breakfast and prepared for the day. A soft blue sun rose over the cabin, evaporating the navy blue night, blending vibrating pastel blues and greens into the forest. I watched from the shadows, awaiting Daniel's return.

Days passed. Daniel tended the garden, mended fences and out buildings, fed the livestock and generally kept the place functional, working with the women in a celebration of a plentiful earth. It was like Daniel had always been there, laboring with them. There was no place for me though and Daniel seemed happy, so I decided to move on. I packed my gear and walked back to the arch, then turned for one last look before I crawled through. Daniel and the women were eating supper on the porch, laughing and talking. I was happy for them but I had to move on. I knelt down to crawl through the arch and saw the gun again, glittering in shadow. I wanted it. I picked it up. I figured it would be okay if I didn't open it and release those little marshmallow creatures that squirmed so cold and pink in my memory. I started through the arch but the gun wouldn't go. I crawled through with my gear and reached back for the gun to pull it through, but it still wouldn't come. So I dropped it and moved on.

A silver corridor appeared, illuminated by a chrome moon circling and polishing the deep blue dome of the sky. The path led through shadows that pressed back the dark trees until it turned into a road. As I walked, the trees along the side of the road grew thinner. The forest faded. Houses appeared, popping up like cartoon mushroom balloons along the side of the road. I walked on and more houses popped up, closer together, until I reached the outskirts of a country town.

Morning broke over a pale blue horizon. Hot-pink highlights stained the gray earth-outline of the sky. I passed a little cottage with a white thigh-high picket fence around the yard. An old woman worked on her flowerbeds. She was soft, gray and ancient like a country grandmother. Her long gray hair was twisted and pinned at the back of her head in a loose bun. A few strands had slipped loose and dangled like feathers at the sides of her neck. Her cheeks were wrinkled with smile lines; her eyes were light blue star-discs in the white sky of her face. She wore a long flower-printed apron over a plain blue cotton dress buttoned up the front. Her stockings were rolled down below her knees and her feet were stuffed into a pair of blocky, black leather shoes. Her ankles puffed out like two fat sausages.

"May I have a drink?" I asked.

"Would you like some lemonade?" She replied. Then she reached under her apron and produced a tall sweating glass, which she handed to me. "Have you been traveling long?" She smiled.

I took a drink. The lemonade was cool and sweet. "Yes, but for the last few weeks I've been camped near a small farm in a clearing by an old stone arch, just down the road."

"I know the place." She said. "Lovely, isn't it, so charming, and such a nice location too. It's a shame it's empty. It would make a beautiful little home for the right family."

"Sorry ma'am, you must be thinking of another place. I was just there. Two young women live there. They have a little farm. A friend of mine took a job as their handy man, I just left them a while ago."

"I'm sorry young man, but I am not mistaken! That house is abandoned, has been for years. No one lives there. A young woman and her daughter lived there a while back, but their hired man shot them one night after supper. He shot himself, too. It was a horrible mess. The postman found the bodies in the morning. The whole town was stunned. He didn't even leave a note. They were such nice girls, too."

I was a little irritated by the old woman's insistence that the house was empty, but she was old. Maybe she just got things mixed up sometimes. "Look lady, I'm sorry but the house is not abandoned. I just left there a while ago." I handed her my empty glass, thanked her and headed back to the arch. I didn't believe her but I had to check out her story. I had to know that Daniel was safe and happy. Houses thinned out and disappeared again as I walked. The trees grew thick, and the pink promise of dawn faded in shadow.

I reached the arch and crawled back through. The silver revolver was gone. Daniel was sitting under a shadowy pine near the arch. He was dirty, smudged and disheveled, like he'd been sleeping on the ground for a long time. His grass-stained face was smeared with mud. Pine needles were embedded in his bushy hair. His elbows rested on his knees. His head hung low as he fiddled with the gun. The cabin was in disrepair, falling down, over-grown and neglected, broken windows stared out like eyes of a ghost. "What happened, Daniel?"

"I don't know. I don't remember. It all happened so fast. It's a long story. I've been waitin' for ya ta get back. I knew y'd come. I wanna go now. I'll tell ya on the way."

"Where are the women?"

"They're gone. I had to shoot 'em."

"What! Why?"

"I don't know. They didn't do anything really. They were just too good, that's all. They loved me too much. I needed their love. I felt like if they ever stopped loving me I wouldn't know what to do. I couldn't take it. I couldn't let go. I knew I'd never be loved like that again. Then I remembered the gun and understood its purpose. It's a gun of love man, not death, a key to doors of souls. So, one night after our meal, I excused myself, walked to the arch and got the gun. When I walked into the dining room and stood in the doorway, they looked at me and saw the gun in my hand. When they saw it, there was no fear in their eyes. They just smiled, stood up, walked into the living room and sat on the couch. Their bright faces were focused on me the whole time. They were still smiling when I pulled the trigger. It was funny though, when the gun went off there was no deafening blast or messy bodies to clean up, they just collapsed inside themselves and became two little balls of light. Wanna see?"

He reached into his shirt pocket and produced two light blue marbles, which he rolled around in the palm his hand. "Can we go now?" he asked. He stood up, walked to the arch and bent down to crawl through but could not pass. The force that blocked the gun blocked his passage as well. "Help me," he said.

"Whatta ya talking about man? Are you crazy? What did ya do? I can't get ya out of this one. An old woman I met in a little village down the road told me about it. I didn't believe her, but it's true. They were innocent. What were you thinking? They were beautiful, you were happy. I don't understand."

"I don't know, man, I just had a vision and followed it. I should'a stayed with you."

"I don't believe this. The old lady said you shot yourself too."

"I don't know, all I remember is after it was over, I wanted to find you but couldn't get through the arch, so I waited. I knew you'd come back. Come on! Help me! Let's go! Let's get outta here!"

"Sorry man, I can't help you this time. There's nothin' I can do. You and the gun are one now an' if the gun can't go through, neither can you. I'd like to help ya, but I can't. You gotta stay an' I gotta go."

He started to say something but stopped. He stood up. We shook hands and I crawled through the arch. I've been walking for days in twilight, never day, never night. And I haven't found the little country town or the old woman yet. I feel Daniel's presence. I glance over my shoulder to see if he is following. Sometimes I spot his shadow scufflin' down the cobwebbed corridors of our history, or stirrin' up puffballs of dust-shadows dancin' on cave walls in my campfire light.

LOBSTER CAT

I was home alone on a long weekend, hangin' around the house with nothin' to do. I listened to a tape of Jack Kerouac reading his poetry to jazz in the background with Steve Allen on piano or Zoot Simms on sax. It sounded so good that I decided to cut a tape of my own. I cleared my kitchen table, a flat boulder in the corner of my kitchen cave, and set up a primal recording studio nestled in a squalor of coffee cups and dishes stacked precariously in the sink. Clothes cluttered rooms, littered with toys haphazardly scattered on the floor, made the living room look like a personal playground my kids carelessly skipped through, watched over by joyful angels that constantly confirmed and blessed the ever-changing harmony of disorder.

I didn't have any musicians for the background music, so I used a small tape player that my wife borrowed from the school where she works for my background music, and my daughter's little Fisher Price toy tape recorder for my voice. I sat at the table for three days, buried in chewed up bones and remains of poetry and audiocassettes. Ashes of mounting cigarette butts spilled from my deep-dish ashtray filled to overflowing and useless. In the end, the recording sounded like it was made with two electronic tin cans strung together on a wire, but I had a good time and filled the tape with poems.

I called this two-bit, low-rent, jam session, "The Basement Tapes," because the recording was so low-down and dirty it reminded me of my basement. I call it a basement but it's really a toxic mud hole in the ground that the original owners built the house over, to hide it because it was so ugly. It's almost all dirt and the only entrance is through a trap door in the bathroom floor that leads down a short narrow flight of beat up, crooked, wooden stairs to a shaky wooden landing resting on wobbly piles of stones stacked in the soft dirt.

When it rains or the ground thaws in the spring, water leaks in and floods the basement, so we have to pump it out. The switch on the sump pump is broken though and we can't afford a new one, so we watch the water level rise to critical, then run down and turn the pump on by hand. That way, the house won't float off its foundation and we can insure the safety of the furnace and hot water heater down there as well. We already lost one water heater in an undiscovered flood, and our well was contaminated in another. We had to dig a new well then, way out in the back yard and well away from that poisoned basement hole.

My house was infested with mice. They entered the bedroom at night and crawled over everything. They crawled on the walls, ceiling and dresser. They hung from the curtains and bedspread, clinging with tiny little claws hooked in the threads of the fabric. They crawled across my face as I slept, tingling little feet scampered over my eyelids.

Every night they came, until I couldn't stand it any more. So, one night, I jumped from bed and found a stick about four or five feet long hidden in a corner. I chased the mice, swinging the stick as I ran. I chased them into the bathroom through the trap door and down the stairs to the basement, but they were too fast and escaped, scurrying down hundreds of little holes in the floor. They came every night after that, and every night I chased them back to their basement holes.

One night though, when I turned to go back to bed, I noticed a larger hole under the stairs that I hadn't seen before. I walked over to investigate. When I reached the hole, something moved inside and a huge lumbering lobster crawled out. It was red, like it was cooked but still alive and moving. Its wet body left a damp trail in the dirt as it crawled. I beat it with my stick until it stopped moving, but I was afraid to pick it up and throw it away. I wanted to wait a few days before I moved the carcass, to make sure it was safe.

The mice came every night after that, and every night I chased them back to their basement holes. Gradually, the lobster carcass turned brown and brittle. When I thought it was safe, I walked over to pick it up. When I touched it, water squirted from the dry joints connecting the sections of the shell. A wet spot spread out in the dirt under the body. The brown shell turned light pink, orange, and then back to red again. It uncurled like a blossoming fire flower and stood up.

The lobster's head had become the head, shoulders, front legs and paws of a cat. It stared at me with runny yellow eyes and crawled in my direction, scraggly cat claws digging in the soft dirt, dragging the armored body behind. The fur on the cat's head was wet and matted down like it had just come in from the rain. Paws and spindly little lobster legs strained under the weight of its heavy shell.

It fixed its runny eyes on me in a sinister stare that stuck me to the floor. Fat pincer claws snapped as it crawled, yellow eyes on me the whole time. It crawled to the wall then up, arching its wet cathead back, upside-down. It crawled across the ceiling over my head, salty eyes on me the whole time, until it reached a wooden box nailed to the ceiling. It crept into the box and disappeared, except for its fanning scaly tail sticking out. Now, whenever I'm in the basement, I keep one eye fixed on that tail. I move quickly and quietly beneath it, so as to not disturb it. I don't want it to chase me anymore.

THE MEETING

I attended a faculty meeting in the auditorium of the high school where I work last night. When I walked in, the principal was speaking from a podium on the stage. When he finished, he introduced me as the next speaker. I didn't know what to do. I wasn't prepared to speak or even dressed properly, in a pair of thread-bare black jeans and faded blue work shirt, wrinkled and open at the neck, no tie, in a beat-up black leather jacket; but I stood up and approached the stage anyway. As I walked, I tried to think of something meaningful to say but couldn't come up with anything. So, when I reached the stairs that led to the podium, I stopped to stall and think. Machine words careened off the inside walls of my skull but I climbed the stairs anyway and hoped for the best.

I reached the podium and graciously greeted the audience, then stood and stared into their shadowy faces in silence. My knees shook. Three-quarters of the crowd stood up and filed out through the double doors in the back of the room, rushing into the alley at the side of the building. I saw them through a row of floor-to-ceiling windows that lined the long left wall of the auditorium. A disturbance had erupted in the alley and a large crowd had gathered to watch. Many of the teachers rushed around the perimeter of the crowd, craning necks and standing on tiptoes to see.

When I spoke, the rest of the audience ran to the windows, pushing, shoving and talking all at once. I felt loose and relaxed then, facing all those empty seats, so I spoke but only babbled strings of disconnected phrases, random nouns and verbs strung together in some cubic Picassian fission. Realizing the futility of my words, I stopped talking and stepped from the stage.

I made polite conversation with a group of teachers who had gathered at the bottom of the stairs waiting for the meeting to come back to order, as the crowd outside continued to mill and swell in the alley. I excused myself and left the auditorium for a cup of coffee and a smoke. A concession stand was set up in a rainbow-striped carnival tent in the lobby. Little, bright, multicolored triangular flags tied to ropes securing the tent poles, flapped wildly in a brisk indoor breeze. I bought a tall cup, black, straight up, from a young man in a white jacket and baseball cap. He didn't speak or smile. His steel-edged stare cut my eyes as he handed me my change. I couldn't move. I leaned against a wall near the door, drank about half a cup and finished my smoke before I returned to the meeting.

When I reached the door of the auditorium, I discovered that a concrete wall with a small metal-framed window in the middle blocked the entrance. I could either climb through the window or find another way around. It was late, so I set my coffee cup on a parlor table under the window and climbed on through, head first, wiggling and struggling. I almost cleared it but my left foot caught on the window frame and I couldn't pull it loose. I dangled helplessly in the stalled space between the floor and window, supporting myself in a handstand pushup position, straining to break the window's unrelenting grip on my shoe. Finally, I broke loose and fell to the floor, stood up, brushed off and reached back through the window for my coffee.

I turned around and discovered I wasn't in the auditorium anymore. I was standing in a well-groomed suburban backyard illuminated with strings of little colored lights strung on poles randomly stuck in the ground, crisscrossing the sky. Tall flaming torches outlined the perimeter of the property. Picnic tables were scattered around the yard, filled with strangers eating, laughing and talking. I sat with a group of six or seven elderly people but wasn't interested in the conversation. I watched the other guests dancing and walking around. Then Trish, a young graduate student I knew, walked over and sat beside me. She was a pretty little Bostonian complete with streetwise razor wit, attitude and accent. She had a small firm body and shoulder-length brown hair. When she sat, her tight gold dress hiked up her right thigh, revealing the soft white curve of her hip slipping from the elastic band of her sheer red panties.

I stared at her exposed cheek and thigh, and when
I looked up she was watching. She smiled and turned away.
I rubbed her bare back. I eased the spaghetti straps of her
dress down the ivory curves of her shoulders. I put my arm
around her and cupped her small breast in my right hand as I
brushed her silky hair aside with the other. I kissed the back
of her long warm neck. She leaned into my kiss for an instant
and moaned. Then she shuddered, jerked away, stood up and
walked into the house.

I decided to go. I walked into the house to thank the
hosts before leaving. I searched the living room, kitchen, den
and basement, but couldn't find them. I wandered down a
long hallway lined with bedrooms. Trish was in one of the
rooms and the door was open. She was naked and kneeling
on the bed, talking to her friend, Melinda, who undressed and
climbed into the bed beside her as they talked.

I walked on down the hall and found the hosts in
the last bedroom. When I walked in, they were humping
away. They sat up when they saw me, sweaty and out of
breath. I thanked them and said goodbye. I passed Trish's and
Melinda's room again on my way out. They were kneeling on
the bed, naked and kissing. Melinda glanced up at me from
her kiss then pressed Trish's honey lips harder to her own.
Her steel stare pierced my vision like thrusting rapiers that
punctured my eyes.

I found the front door, walked to my car parked
at the curb, climbed in and drove down a concrete street
winding through a ranch-style suburban neighborhood. Neat,
evenly spaced houses lined both sides of the street. I passed a
hitchhiker, thumb out under a streetlight, and picked him up.
He was tall and thin, a young man with wire-rimmed glasses and
long greasy blond hair. His clothes were filthy and wrinkled. He
smelled like hard times, cigarettes and beer. He had a wild look
in his eye. He sat in the passenger's seat staring straight ahead,
mumbling angry curses to the night. The road blurred and I
blacked out.

When I came to, I wasn't driving anymore. I was sitting
cross-legged on a living room floor across from the hitchhiker.
A fat little naked baby was lying on its stomach between us. The
young man loved the baby. I could tell by the way he looked at
it, talked to it and touched it. I loved the baby too. I wanted to
make it laugh. I leaned over and patted the baby's white little
butt like a bongo drum. The baby laughed but the hitchhiker
became angry. He tried to smash my nose into my face with the
palm of his hand, but I blocked his strike and redirected his arm
as I leaned away.

He looked at me and spoke with a trembling voice,
explaining how dangerous it was to get cut on the eyebrow.
"There's a major artery there," he said, "an' if ya get cut there,
someone could pinch it an' pull it out. Then ya'd bleed ta
death." As he spoke, he pinched his eyebrow with his thumb

and forefinger and pulled an artery out about six inches from his head, then let it go. It snapped back like a slimy rubber band and I blacked out again.

I awoke this morning in my own bed, rolled over, scratched my chest and shook my head, showered, shaved, gulped down a tall cup of coffee and inhaled a last cigarette before I headed to school.

COMMANDO

Shotgun, Gene and I stopped in Chicago on our way home to Cleveland on the last lap of our cross-country trip. We wanted to spend some late-night time drinkin' in a blues bar, so we parked the car in a commuter lot north of town and took a train to Michigan Avenue. An old black man in a worn wool overcoat an' stockin' hat was blowin' harmonica for tips outside the station. He was good. A small crowd had gathered to listen. I gave him five bucks an' said, "We're from outta town an' wanna hear some good Blues. You know a place?"

"Well, that'd be the south side son, but it can get rough down there if you ain't hip. Be careful."

"We're okay. Where can we go? You know a good place?"

"Well, let me see, Little Rosie's, yeah, that's a good place for you boys, just a few blocks down Michigan, then two blocks south and left on Drexel. Rosie's is right there on the corner. She'll take good care o' you boys."

"Thanks man, have a good one."

"Yeah, you too." He said. Then he winked, tapped his foot for a beat and leaned back into his harp.

Shotgun, Gene and I had been friends for a long time and we'd been in a lot o' scrapes together in many saloons. They were fearless fighters. Shotgun was short and stocky with stubby meaty hands and stringy blond hair draped over his broad, denim-clad, shoulders. His beard was a thick blond shield over his chest. He was a little bow-legged in tight-patched jeans, but walked with a purpose in heavy engineer boots like a bulldog loose on the street. Gene was tall, muscular and handsome with neat-cut long black hair, Wild Bill Hickok moustache and goatee in designer jeans and a tight black T-shirt. They were bar fighters and were usually the ones who started the fight, with drunken tempers eruptin' over nothin', but they always cleaned out the place and got away without a scratch.

We followed the old man's directions but got lost along the river. We stalked abandoned streets, block-to-block, looking for Little Rosie's. We asked for help in an endless number of parks, churches, restaurants, warehouses, and department stores but no one had ever heard of the place. We gave up and headed back to Michigan Avenue. Shotgun picked up a pint of Bourbon at a liquor store for the walk.

"I say, we head back to the river and take a right," Gene said, as he hit on the bottle and passed it to me. "I think downtown's that way."

Shotgun shrugged his shoulders. "Okay with me" he said.

I took a big hit off the bottle. " I don't know what to do. We gotta find a subway someplace and get back to the car. I wanna get outta here. This ain't workin'."

We walked a few more blocks searchin' for a train with no idea of which train we needed to take or where to go to catch it. So, we ducked down the first greasy subway tunnel we came to and boarded the first train that came along, hopin' it was headed in the right direction. The train clicked through many stops but not the stop we needed.

"Come on guys, let's just get off at the next stop and take our chances," Shotgun said. Then he slugged on the bottle and passed it around.

When the train rolled into the next stop and the doors hissed open, we stepped off. Newspapers, candy wrappers, Styrofoam cups, old sandwiches and doughnuts littered the concrete floor and benches. We found the exit to the street and climbed another gritty stairway to a dingy neighborhood on the outskirts of town.

"Go right," I said, "I think I see a light." We walked on, passin' the bottle around until it was empty. The stiletto vibration of our clicking heels on the pavement echoed down a desolate brownstone canyon. Streetlights burned out, poppin' sparks over our heads as we passed under them, sprinklin' tinglin' splinters o' glass on the stained pavement behind us. Apartment houses with broken windows stared out from both sides of the street.

We passed an old Victorian house that was well groomed, neat, white, and so misplaced in that gritty corner of the city. When we passed, a red neon sign blinked on in a picture window in the middle of the long clapboard wall of the porch. "Little Rosie's" it flashed. Muffled, low-down slow drivin' blues drifted from a green screen door at the top of the stairs leadin' to the porch.

"Here we are. Let's grab a couple o' beers." Shotgun said.

"Yeah, I'm with ya." Gene grinned. "Let's sit for a while."

"Okay guys, but I don't want any trouble, ya hear! Just a couple o' quick ones, an' we go, understand?"

They agreed, so we climbed the stairs an' stepped through the door. Hypnotic three-cord blues rhythms drifted from a chrome jukebox glowin' smoky red and blue neon lights in a dark corner of the room. The place was packed with old men sittin' and drinkin' the smoke-filled night away as steel blues passed like shots of bourbon before them.

The only women in the place were three young waitresses and an old gray barmaid. When we walked in, two of the waitresses were escortin' a young white girl out the door sayin', "This ain't no place fo' you, honey, so shake it." We found three stools at the bar an' sat down. The old barmaid walked over, "How ya doin' boys? I'm Rosie, what can I getcha?"

"We'll have a round o' drafts." I said. " I'll cover it."

"Comin' right up boys, I'll be right back."

Gene turned to an old guy slouched over the bar next to him and said, "How ya doin'?" The guy didn't look up at Gene or even acknowledge his presence. He just stared at the wall an' sipped his half-empty glass. Rosie brought our beers and we sat on our stools starrin' at the wall too; three ghosts at the end of the smoky bar, drinkin' an' studyin' the lean brownstone faces of the other men drinkin' the night away. Rosie walked over and said, "Be patient boys. Have another beer. You gotta ride comin'."

"Whadda ya mean?" I asked. But Rosie just smiled an' walked away.

Shotgun, Gene and I drank until their heads crashed on the bar. "Okay guys," I said, "let's step outside for some air." I helped 'em up, out the door and down the porch stairs but they passed out on the front lawn. I dragged them under a bush and covered them with two worn blankets I found folded under a tree, and then stumbled back to my stool to wait for our ride. I had a few more beers. One by one, the other men drifted through the door an' into the night, until I was the only one left in the bar, floatin' peacefully on the smooth heat of alcohol an' blues.

Rosie stepped from behind the bar an' walked toward me, swaying heavy hips like a slim young girl on the make, a bizarre cross between a warm-hug grandmother and a hot slut. She leaned against the bar. "I'm the ride you been waitin' fo', honey. I know whatcha want and where ya wanna go."

"Thanks" I said as I hugged her.

"Oh, come on honey, is that all the sugar ya got fo' me?" She grabbed my groin and squeezed. She smiled an' I noticed she had no teeth. "I got what ya need right here, baby," she said. Then, she stepped away from the bar, spread her legs and hiked up her skirt, liftin' it, gradually exposing the great brown mass of her thighs an' thick bulge of her waist. A set of false teeth chattered wildly in the dark crease of the coarse pocket of her womanhood. The jukebox blared some slow drivin', hard grindin' blues and Rosie swayed her huge hips, bumpin' and grindin'. "This way baby, follow me," she said, "it's right in here." Then she stepped through a worn wool blanket hanging over a doorway and vanished into a dark backroom.

The music was so hot I followed. On the way, I passed a broken window that looked onto the street. Shredded plastic strips covered the shattered panes. Warm night breezes fluttered the strips. I glanced out the window as I passed and saw a young white couple in black patent-leather leotards jazz dancin' in the street to the cool blues comin' from the bar. Pastel rainbow flowers ignited around their feet as they moved. They fired machine-guns into the darkness behind them as they danced past the bar. I looked back down the street and saw a platoon of young white soldiers outfitted in full camouflage gear, chasin' the dancers. They carried machine guns and fired in the direction of the jazz couple as they ran. Light-flower sparks ignited around the dancers' feet where the bullets hit.

I remembered Shotgun and Gene under the bush outside, exposed and vulnerable. I rushed through the door. The platoon spread out and sprayed the area. Bullets blazed past me. I dodged and darted until I reached them. They were just comin' to. "Let's go!" I screamed, "We gotta get outta here!"

"What's up?" Shotgun asked.

"We got big trouble. There're soldiers firin' guns all around us. Move."

They crawled out. We stood up an' ran along a six-foot brick wall around the property, crouchin' low to make smaller targets. We cut an' darted around the side of the house but were trapped. The soldiers had surrounded Little Rosie's. We took a chance an' headed for the street, but got caught in a crossfire on the front lawn in a helicopter spotlight that scanned the bar. We ducked and dodged as bullets whizzed past our heads and feet. Pastel hell-flowers ignited wherever the bullets hit. Then Shotgun ran into the street and Gene and I followed. We cut and darted but there was no way out, so we stopped and raised our hands. The firing stopped like someone threw a switch. In the deafening silence, a silhouette of a commando appeared on the flat rooftop of a two-story warehouse across the street. A rocket launcher was perched on his shoulder like a predator bird waiting to strike. "Who's that guy?" Gene said. "What're we gonna do?"

"I don't know," I said, "duck an' cover, I guess, duck an' cover."

The commando dropped to one knee and aimed the rocket in our direction. When he fired, we hit the dirt, face down, bodies pressed flat to the ground with our heads buried in our arms. The sound of the explosion an' the force of the concussion struck me at the same time as Little Rosie's rose in a ball of flame.

I looked up. The soldiers were gone. "Let's go!" I yelled. We stood up and ran but stopped when we saw the commando standin' in our path. He was big, grimy, unshaven and sweaty, chewin' on the filthy stub of a cigar. He smiled, knelt down and aimed again in our direction. He had us good and he knew it. He grinned as he squeezed the trigger.

MY NEIGHBOR

The great lake was steel blue and so huge I couldn't see the other shore. Waves methodically rolled onto the beach. The days were hot, glorious, endless and clear. Our house was located about a hundred yards from the water. White sand reached all the way to the rough wooden stairs of our long front porch. The house was two stories tall, weather-beaten white with faded green-shuttered windows.

Our neighbors' house was just like ours but built on a large dune about fifty yards down the beach. A boy lived there with his family. He had a massive body, strong and muscular like a weight lifter or a hard-working farm boy, big enough to be mistaken for a man, but his head was only the size of a baseball. All day long he sat on his front steps staring at the lake, uncomfortably shifting his enormous body in the unforgiving heat. The boy's face was distorted with wrinkles, as if at one time his head had been a normal size but somehow shrunk, leaving all the excess skin folded around a much smaller skull.

His features were pushed together like a chubby little prune. It was impossible to distinguish where his eyes, nose, lips and ears were. He wore heavy wool trousers held up by thick suspenders, even on the hottest days, and a long-sleeved work shirt buttoned up to his thin little neck. I felt sorry for him and visited him often. Our conversations were so one-sided though, because I was the only one who ever talked. I chattered the day away as he watched the water.

One day, a stranger arrived in a powerful speedboat. He pulled up to a quick stop at the end of the long pier. Choppy water slapped the shore. He tied his boat to the pier and ran wildly onto the beach, laughing, waving his arms, flipping and jumping, holding a tall black stovepipe hat to the top his head. His body was thin and wiry. His arms and legs were like pipe cleaners or tentacles attached to an only slightly thicker torso. He wore a long black heavy coat over a black shirt and vest. His black pants were tucked into the tops of knee-high black leather boots. His facial features were angular and sharp, a handlebar moustache curled up to his eyebrows. He moved as if he were a silent movie villain rushing like a spider-shadow across the sand. The stranger ran to the steps where my neighbor was sitting as I watched from the shore. He jabbed a long bony finger at the boy, laughing, mocking him and calling him names.

"Hey pinhead!" he said, "Yeah, you with the ballpoint head an' face like a raisin! I'm talkin' to you!"

He insulted the boy's looks and intelligence, his father's manhood and mother's virtue, as he kept poking that bone-for-a-finger in the boy's small face.

The attack had no effect on the boy though. He just sat on the step staring at the lake, apparently void of any fear, anger, or hatred, never moving or saying a word, content to be alone with the sand, heat and cool eternity of the lake rising and falling against the pale blue length of the horizon.

Who is this guy anyway? I wondered *Why is he terrorizing this boy?* I didn't know what his problem was but I didn't care for his methods. Maybe the boy had cheated him at cards or crossed him in a business deal. Maybe he hurt the guy's wife or family or somehow scandalized the guy's well-earned good name. If he did, I'm sure he didn't mean to. After all, his head was only the size of a baseball. How much calculated damage could he do?

I ran to the house to help the boy but I was too far away and the sand was too loose and deep. My feet turned to stones. I sank up to my knees in the sand with every step and the house didn't get any closer. I screamed at the guy to leave my friend alone, but my futile rescue attempts didn't concern him at all. He just increased his taunting as if I wasn't even there.

When I reached the porch, the stranger laughed and dashed off, wildly flipping and jumping across the sand again, back to his boat. He fired up the engine and sped away, circling in front of the pier; churning water crashed waves onto the beach before he shot off to the horizon, leaving me stuck and knee-deep in sand. He came often after that, but always when I was too far away to help.

I was sitting on the beach one day, watching the sunset, thinking about how I could help my friend, when a white seagull landed beside me. It walked around, cawing at the sky. I fed it some bread. It flew away and flew back a few minutes later with a talisman hanging from its bill. The talisman was made of a clamshell with a shiny blue stone set in the middle. The shell was wrapped with an intricately woven ring of seaweed and feathers hanging from an ornately knotted sea-vine. The gull dropped the necklace at my feet, cawed and flew away. I put the talisman around my neck as the bird flapped into the horizon.

The next day, the stranger came screaming into the bay in his boat again, and again danced down the pier across the sand and up to the porch. But when he started his insults, I rose above the sand and floated toward the house like a ghost across the beach, before the stranger realized I was there. He looked up. We were face-to-face, eye to jaundiced eye, and he began to spin a black whirlwind whipping sand in my face. He flipped across the sand to the pier again, jumped into his boat, started the engine and took off, circling the bay and crashing waves onto the shore before shooting off into the sun. He came often after that, but always when I was too far away to help. I managed to chase him away each time though, flipping back to his boat. The talisman was just a piece of the puzzle. I was the rest.

We went home in August and the following summer my parents sold the beach house, so I never saw my friend again. I only see him in my mind now; sitting on his step like a prince on a front-porch throne, content to contemplate the glittering blue distance of the lake's easy waves slapping the blistered shore.

THE PRIEST

I was a priest once and had a small parish in the country. It was the end of June. Summer days were hot but cool breezes blew, soothing and smoothing the leaves and long grass in the meadows, perfect weather for our monthly sacrifice. We performed the selection ceremony and chose a member of the congregation as the offering. We also chose the alternate. Unfortunately, the Chosen One had an important appointment to keep on Endings Day, with his insurance agent, stockbroker, lawyer or something, and the alternate had to visit his mother.

Someone suggested we move the sacrifice ahead by a day and have two sacrifices in July, but most of the congregation felt that changing the sacred day to the next month was completely unacceptable. The sacrifice had always been held on the last day of the month. It was an important symbolic reminder of the endings of things. To change the day would shake the very foundations of our belief.

As our spiritual leader, it was my job to find a suitable replacement. I didn't know what to do. We'd never lost both the Chosen One and the alternate at the same time. Usually, one of them was available. And I'd never been in a position of having to choose to send a member of our congregation to their death. The selection ceremony was designed to choose an offering through a ritual process of a secret accidental consensus of the members of the Endings Committee. In that way, no individual member of the committee could be held responsible for the choice. We all carried the same blame and absolution equally. There were too many cosmic factors involved in a decision like that, and they were far too complicated for my meager mind to adequately comprehend.

"Look," I said, "I don't know how to pick anyone. I don't know how to choose. I'll ask for a volunteer and if no one comes forward, I'll do it myself."

This was a risky move on my part, but I had faith in the compassionate generosity of my people. The committee agreed to my plan. I called the congregation together and explained the situation. Then I asked for a volunteer and we waited. A long silence followed, thick as the heat. No one responded. I was nervous. I scanned the crowd for a hand. Finally, one appeared in the back of the church and a young man stepped from the crowd. I didn't know him. I asked him his name and where he lived.

"I am here now," he said, "staying with friends. My name isn't important."

"Are you sure you want to do this?" I asked.

"Why not? What's the difference? Everybody dies. I'll just take an earlier place in line if it'll help. Seems like a good way to go, that's all. I'll see you at the sacrifice." Then he turned and left the church.

The days leading to Endings Day crept slowly until the holy day arrived. The church buzzed with activity as the congregation prepared for the celebration. I went to my dressing room to put on my ceremonial robe and hat but I couldn't find them. I tore the place apart. I was in a hurry. I wanted to get the sacrifice over with. I didn't want to waste any time. How could I misplace a huge gold embroidered purple hat and robe? I put on my purple and gold down vest and baseball cap instead, which seemed perfectly appropriate for a little country ritual.

When I walked into the great hall, everyone was preparing for the day. Knives were sharpened and ornate vessels of holy water were placed around the altar. Sponges and mops waited in dozens of steaming buckets of hot soapy water. The members of the congregation were dressed in their sacrificial best. The laughter of children at play filled the church as we waited for the Chosen One to arrive. Then, a messenger ran into the room and announced that the Chosen One would not be coming. During the night, he had run off to give his life for some other holy war in another place, and again, we had no offering.

I asked for a volunteer and waited. A silent moment passed. No one stepped forward. Time ticked, hands clicked and stopped, until I gave in and volunteered. I said I would do it. I couldn't go back on my word. How could I order anyone to die if I wasn't prepared to die myself? But I wasn't ready. I had things to do. I had to wash the car, feed the cat, pick up the wine, pay the bills and relax a little bit. I was thinking about these things when the honor guard formed around me and marched me up the white marble stairs to the altar.

The conflict between my guilt for failing the congregation and my desire to live rang like a Sunday mission bell in my head. Out of the corner of my eye, I noticed that the back door of the church was right next to the altar door. If I hit one of the guards in the gut with my elbow and side-kicked the other one in the knee, I could bolt through the door, slam it behind me and get a good head start. There were plenty of other jobs in plenty of other towns, I didn't need this one. But how could I run out on my fine people? I was their spiritual guide.

I stopped, puzzled and confused. It reminded me of a story I read in high school about a guy who circumstantially found himself in a position of having to choose to open one of two doors. Behind one door was a beautiful young woman. If he opened it, he would marry her, inherit a fortune and go free. Behind the other, a tiger waited to tear him to shreds and eat him. At the end of the story, the guy was looking at the doors, trying to decide, "Door number one or door number two?" And just like that guy, I never found out which door I opened.

ABOUT THE AUTHOR

Jeff Bender was born a coal miner's son in Richwood, West Virginia. He migrated to Ohio with his family when he was five years old. He wrote his first poem in 1966, in an attic apartment in Mt. Clemens, Michigan and has been writing poetry, stories and essays ever since. He attended Kent State University and was a protester in 1970 when the shootings occurred. He migrated to Vermont in the mid 70's and found a peaceful environment in which to write, and raise a family. He has four children; Kim, Jason, Sibyl and Dylan. He has been a factory worker, construction worker, tax appraiser, human service worker, community organizer, waiter, salesman and factory owner, as well as a teacher. He brings all of these experiences to his writing. He has organized and conducted writing workshops and poetry readings in the Rutland area for many years. He currently teaches seventh grade writing and ancient history at Rutland Town School in Rutland Town, Vermont. He has read his poetry and stories in many venues throughout Vermont and was awarded writing Fellowships from the National Writing Project and Vermont Studio Center.

www.ingramcontent.com/pod-product-compliance
Lightning Source LLC
Chambersburg PA
CBHW031607260626
47154CB00020B/1702